PINEAPPLE GINGERBREAD MEN

A Pineapple Port Mystery: Book Seven

Amy Vansant

ISBN-9781730918971
Library of Congress: 2018911988

Vansant Creations, LLC / Amy Vansant
Annapolis, MD
http://www.AmyVansant.com
http://www.PineapplePort.com

Copy editing by Carolyn Steele.
Proofreading by Effrosyni Moschoudi, Connie Leap & Meg Barnhart

CHAPTER ONE

Kristopher Rudolph poured himself another bourbon as the dog in his bathroom launched into its fifteenth chorus of *Yap Yourself a Merry Little Christmas*. The miserable little rat-creature would not *shut up*. He heard it trying to scratch a hole through the door and grunted, pleased he had no intention of trying to recover his damage deposit anyway.

The worst part was the noise. It sounded more like the dog was trying to dig a hole through his *skull* than the door.

How a dog the size of a football could make that kind of racket—

"Shut up!"

Grabbing a bag of pretzels from his kitchen counter, Kris tore it open and pounded down the hall. He cracked open the bathroom door and used his ankle to block the tiny dog's escape as he slipped in his hand, inverted the bag, and shook it.

Pretzels rained. Startled, the Yorkshire terrier backed away from the door, looking like a long-haired toupee with eyes.

Kris glared at it. "There, you happy? You are going home tomorrow. I *promise*."

He shut the door.

Silence.

Well, *munching*, but that was better than barking.

Kris took a deep breath and patted his round tummy, suddenly craving pretzels. He strode back up the hall, shoved the empty pretzel bag into the kitchen garbage, grabbed a bourbon, and toted it to his overstuffed chair to park himself in front of the television. As a commercial for reverse mortgages blared, his gaze swept over his living room decorations.

Strips of lights lined the ceiling like disco crown molding. A Christmas tree stood beside him, blinking with frenetic urgency—middle section, bottom section, top section—over and over, sending semaphore messages to the reindeer, sleighs, and giant snowmen flashing their own secrets from his front yard. A full set of reindeer ran across the wall above his sofa. Rudolph led the way. At least fifty other Rudolphs grinned from table tops and tissue box cozies.

He groaned and took a sip of his bourbon. "Freakin' Christmas."

Thanks to his last name, people around the little swamp town he currently called home were always gifting him Rudolphs, thinking they were clever.

The presents were about as clever as sending someone from Maine a lobster mug.

I should be happy. Celebrating.

He took another sip of his bourbon and tried to concentrate on his upcoming retirement.

Somewhere warm. Somewhere they've never heard of Christmas. Somewhere they've never even heard of December.

Perched on at least six other flat surfaces, tiny stuffed elves stared at him with disapproving sideward glances, their arms crossed over their knees.

Kris winked at one as he sipped his drink. "Yeah, yeah, I've been naughty."

His shoulder muscles had just begun to unbunch when his doorbell rang, and Jingle Bells sang throughout the house.

The dog began to bark anew.

Kris closed his eyes, searching for strength. Not only did he have to answer the door, but he had to pretend he enjoyed the company.

One more month, and this hell will be over.

Setting down his bourbon, he stood and opened the front door.

Crowded in his doorway stood two poofy gingerbread men. Leaning to the left and tilting his head to the side, he found two more behind the first pair. He recognized the costumes from the Charity Christmas parade earlier that day. The gingerbread men had been running around, as gingerbread men were wont to do. The curious part was *he* organized the parade, and *he* hadn't booked any gingerbread men. At the time, he hadn't thought much about it. It wasn't unusual for people wearing silly costumes to join in a parade unannounced, especially in these Podunk little towns where half the locals' bloodlines intersected. But he had to admit, now that the cookies were standing on his doorstep, his curiosity had been piqued.

He pulled at his enormous white beard and did his best to look jolly.

"My, my, look at you all. How can I help you?"

The foremost gingerbread shoved him with two caramel-colored mitted hands. Unprepared, Kris stumbled backward, hands flailing to regain his balance. Bourbon splashed across the wall, and his glass sailed through the air.

"We want what we're owed," said one of the cookies as they piled into his house. He couldn't tell which one. Their mouths didn't move.

CHAPTER TWO

Earlier That Day

"Ooh! Here come those little cars," said Mariska, pointing.

Older men, each with a red fez on his head, appeared driving tiny orange cars, weaving back and forth across the parade route as if the vehicles themselves had spent the day drinking.

Darla scowled. "Who are they? What do little cars have to do with Christmas?"

"They're Shriners. It's a club for men."

"What isn't?" muttered Darla.

Charlotte chuckled and looked at her watch. It was nearly Christmas, and she had a lot to do. Back at her house, an enormous embroidery machine waited patiently in her shed, eager to stitch Schnauzers and Cavalier King Charles Spaniels on golf head covers and polo shirts. Helping Mariska's son and daughter-in-law with their pet embroidery business had once been Charlotte's only job.

Now, she was officially a private investigator.

But with the holidays rapidly approaching, the crimes had dwindled, and the demand for Dachshunds on kitchen towels had gone up, and she'd agreed to help for one last holiday.

She glanced at the two older ladies beside her.

That is if Mariska ever lets me get any work done.

Charlotte's adoptive mother had *insisted* she come watch the parade. After she'd been orphaned as a girl, Mariska, her husband Bob and Darla—with the help of Darla's husband, Sheriff Frank—had arranged it so Charlotte could grow up in their fifty-five-plus community, Pineapple Port. If it hadn't been for them, after the death of her grandmother, Charlotte would have been whisked off as a ward of the state. Shuffled through the system, she would have had a very different upbringing.

As it was, picking up some of their 'retiree habits' way too young was the worst that had happened to her. Most twenty-seven-year-olds didn't go to water aerobics or watch television with the closed-captioning on.

She had work to do, and Mariska had insisted she go to a parade. *Oh well.* In the grand scheme of things, it seemed like a small price to pay.

"Why do we have a parade again?" she asked over the pounding of a local high school's marching band. There hadn't been a Christmas parade in Charity, the city that housed Pineapple Port, since she was a little girl.

"You can thank Kristopher Rudolph. The man who looks like Santa," called back Mariska.

Charlotte's brow knit as she pictured the man. Whenever she'd seen him, she couldn't help but think his big white beard made for a poor facial hair choice in steamy Florida. It made her scratch her chin just thinking about it. "When did he move to Pineapple Port? Last summer, right?"

Mariska nodded, her auburn curls bouncing. "This is what he does. He arranges big Christmas events for towns to help them raise money for charity."

"The man is *obsessed*," chimed in Darla. "I had to deliver a cake to him for his charity bake sale, and his house looks like this whole parade just marched right in there and took a seat."

Charlotte shrugged. "I guess with a name like Kristopher Rudolph..."

"I know *three* women who bought him Rudolph the red-nosed reindeer statues," said Mariska as four gingerbread men ran by, slapping kids' outstretched hands with their own puffy mitts. "They put no thought at all into it."

Darla hooked a thumb in Mariska's direction. "She took him a homemade jar of *Rudolph the Red Pepper Jelly.*"

Mariska nodded. "*That* was clever. Man needs another statue like he needs another whisker in his beard."

Darla winked at Charlotte. "Kris is single, and he likes fruit cake. The ladies in Pineapple Port have been waiting *years* for a man like that to show up."

Mariska's eyes flashed. "I wasn't *flirting* with him."

"Not you. *You* just have way too much homemade pepper jelly in your cabinets."

Mariska's expression relaxed, and she giggled. "I do. It's true. I think we overdid it this year."

Mariska gasped and pointed, nearly taking out the eye of the woman next to her. "There he is now."

With the blaring of sirens, a fire truck inched down Main Street, a jolly Santa perched on top, waving. Teenage girls dressed like elves grabbed handfuls of candy from red and green buckets and tossed treats into the crowd.

Charlotte looked at her watch again. "That's the end, right?"

"Of course it is. Santa's always last. Haven't you ever seen a Christmas parade before?"

"I grew up *here*, remember? I was about six the last time we had a Christmas parade."

"Don't be a Grinch. What are you in a hurry to get back to?"

"I have about twenty orders to stitch, and Aggie Mae lost her Yorkie, Pudding. I promised I'd help her look for him."

Darla rolled her eyes. "That little thing's in a gator's belly by now. You'll notice there aren't a lot of packs of wild Yorkies roaming Florida. I'm surprised he lived this long."

Mariska smacked her friend's shoulder. "That's terrible."

Darla shrugged. "Terrible but true."

CHAPTER THREE

It was nearly ten p.m. when Charlotte received a call from Sheriff Frank. She had to look at her clock a second time to be sure she wasn't imagining the hour as she fumbled to answer. This was the equivalent of two a.m. in a retirement community.

"Is everything okay?" she asked, in lieu of a more traditional greeting.

"You said you wanted me to give you a ring next time I had a murder investigation. Wanted me to walk you through the scene. Still interested?"

"Ooh!" Charlotte sat up, excited. Abby, her soft-coated Wheaten terrier, stretched and kicked the side of her leg, cranky the phone had woken her as well.

Charlotte had forgotten she'd asked Frank to give her a call the next time he had a body. She wanted more experience with crime scenes and figured her inside track with the local sheriff could come in handy. "Yes, definitely. Where are you?"

"A few blocks away."

"In Pineapple Port?"

"Yup."

"Oh no. Who?"

"Kristopher Rudolph."

"The parade Santa?"

"Uh huh."

Charlotte wiped the sleepies from her eyes and took a moment to think. Her brain hadn't quite caught up with her mouth yet.

"Did he have a heart attack or something?" She wasn't sure how much she'd learn by peering at death by natural causes, and her pillow suddenly felt extra comfortable.

Frank snorted a laugh. "No. It's fishy, all right. You'll see when you get here. You know the address?"

She nodded and then realized he couldn't see her response. "Yes. I think so."

"We'll be hard to miss. Follow the flashing lights."

"Okay. I'll be there in a second."

Charlotte threw on shorts and a t-shirt while Abby watched her from the bed. The dog's eyes slid shut and then sprang open again and again, torn between keeping vigil and sleeping.

"Heaven forbid you miss anything," said Charlotte, petting the dog's belly. Abby's leg swiveled like the hand on a clock to give her access to better rubbing. "It's okay. Nothing you have to worry about. You get your beauty sleep, princess."

Abby grunted and centered herself on her back, her lower legs falling open to either side in a very unladylike fashion. She seemed unconcerned with Charlotte's unusual nighttime departure. There'd been a time Abby would *never* have allowed mommy to leave without an escort, but Charlotte guessed she'd left the house and come back *alive* enough times now that Abby took her eventual return for granted.

Charlotte left her house and jogged toward Kristopher Rudolph's. Though all the modular homes in Pineapple Port shared similarities, there'd be no mistaking Kristopher's this evening. Two sheriff's vehicles, one with lights flashing in silence, sat parked outside. A small crowd of neighbors and gossips encircled the residence, murmuring to one another as they shared wild conjecture about the scene inside.

A Yorkshire terrier, tethered to the same style of head-high, white lamp post that stood sentry outside all the homes in Pineapple Port, yapped in a steady staccato beat as Charlotte approached. She squatted and lifted his chin to stare into his shiny eyes.

"Pudding, what are you doing out here?" She looked for Aggie Mae but didn't see her in the crowd. "Looks like you're not in an alligator's belly after all."

The dog celebrated by continuing to bark.

The front door of the home's porch banged open, and she heard Frank bark in his own gruff baritone. "Get in here."

"Do I get credit for finding Pudding?" asked Charlotte, scurrying up the stairs. The crowd whispering behind her hissed to a crescendo. Now *she* had become part of the speculation.

I'll tell them I was brought in as a consultant.

She giggled at the idea.

Charlotte Morgan: Crime Consultant.

She needed to get a sash and patches made like a Girl Scout. Private Eye patch, *check*. Crime Consultant patch, *check*.

Frank stared at the dog, frowning. "Pudding? Isn't that Aggie Mae's dog?"

"Yep. He'd gone missing. She asked me to be on the lookout."

"Mission accomplished."

Frank held open the screen door for her, and Charlotte eyed his outfit. He wore a thin, light blue robe over a t-shirt and boxers. His sheriff's hat sat perched on ruffled tufts of uncombed hair. The robe hung to his knees and was held shut by the gun belt encircling his middle.

"Nice outfit."

Frank grunted. "I had to get over here quick."

"Using the gun belt as a sash, bold choice."

"At least I remembered the hat."

"Isn't that Darla's robe?"

"Shush up and get in here."

Chuckling, Charlotte crossed the front porch to enter the double-wide modular home. The interior door had been propped open with a ceramic snowman the size of a golden retriever.

Charlotte smelled smoke as she approached, and as Frank entered and stepped to the right, she caught her first glimpse as to why.

A fat gingerbread man costume—presumably with someone inside—sat in a large padded reclining chair. The edges of the costume had been licked by flames, leaving black smudges as if the baker had left him in the oven too long.

"Here's our burnt cookie," said Frank, pulling the head off the costume. Beneath it, Charlotte recognized the tufted white beard of Kristopher Rudolph, Pineapple Port's new Mr. Christmas. His blue eyes stared back at her as if his fate had somehow been her fault.

"He was Santa at the parade this morning," she mumbled to no one. Something near the man's mouth had her hypnotized.

Another set of eyes.

Is that an elf...?

Squinting, she moved forward, her hand reaching toward the dead man.

"Is that an elf peeking out of his mouth?"

"Don't touch." Frank slapped her hand lightly, and she retracted it, eyes never leaving the saucy elf peeking at her from faux-Santa's lips.

"How—"

"Near as we can tell, he choked on the legs. Those little things have long legs, y'know." Frank paused and then shook his head. "If this is what happens when those elves find out you've been naughty, I've been underestimating them for years..."

Charlotte yanked away her gaze. It wasn't easy, and she knew she'd never see an elf again without picturing it being gobbled by Santa.

She glanced at a pile of ash beneath the Christmas tree. "I'd assumed the fire killed him, but—?"

"Nope. He got lucky there, so to speak. The tree was fire retardant, and what might have looked like a good enough blaze to cover the evidence died soon after it was set. You'd think the place would've gone up like a tinder box with all this crap in here."

Frank made a sweeping motion with his arm, and Charlotte's eye followed. The gingerbread man, elf, and fire ash had captured her attention—she'd almost missed the insanity of the room's décor. Christmas decorations hung, sat, or leaned against every inch.

"Kind of a *live by the sword, die by the sword* sort of thing," she said, counting the room's thirteenth Rudolph the red-nosed reindeer trinket.

Frank grunted. "What's that?"

"Lived for Christmas, died by elf."

"Hm. Poetic."

Charlotte squat to poke at the ash on the ground. Near the back of the tree, one of the packages had only partially burned. Using a half-melted candy cane, she hooked it and pulled it towards her. The side crumbled, revealing the smooth bottom of an empty cardboard box.

"The gifts are empty."

Frank hung his thumbs in his belt. "They're burned."

"No, this one back here is only a bit burned. It was empty." Charlotte stood and pointed at the pile of ash. "There aren't any lumps that might have been gifts here. They were *all* empty boxes."

"So? They were there for show."

"I suppose, but...that's *weird*."

"Why?"

"Well, think about it. When Darla trots out all her

decorations, does she set fake packages under the tree?"

"No. She puts all the crap she bought with my hard-earned money around it until she gets a chance to give them out to a bunch of people who aren't *me*."

"Exactly. If you're not a store, why would you stage your Christmas tree? It doesn't look like he has anyone to gift—" she glanced at Kris Rudolph and then looked away, feeling as if the elf in his mouth had caught her peeking. "Can we put his head back on?"

Frank reached for the gingerbread man's head and slipped it over Kristopher's. "No problem. That's why it was back on in the first place. Daniel couldn't stop laughing. Tried to take a picture for his instant graham cracker."

"Instagram."

"Whatever. Look—" Frank's gaze pinballed around the room as if he feared someone could overhear them. "I know I called you down here because you asked me to share this stuff, but that wasn't the only reason I called you."

"No?"

"No. I'm under a lot of pressure with this one, and I'm surrounded by morons with the maturity level of five-year-olds—"

"You mean Deputy Daniel."

"Of course I mean Deputy Daniel. Bottom line is I need someone I can *trust*. Someone with a good mind for this stuff. Daniel's brain is preoccupied with online gaming and his doll collection."

"He collects action figures."

"Dolls in tights. Same thing."

Charlotte pursed her lips to keep from smiling.

He trusts me. He thinks I'm good at this.

She wanted to crow. She wanted to hug Frank for trusting her and, even more so, for *admitting* he trusted her. Frank guarded his affections like a national treasure.

Be calm.

She cleared her throat. "But what makes this investigation special?"

"Harlan is going to want answers."

"The mayor?"

Frank nodded and motioned to the gingerbread man. "This guy was a big deal."

"How so?"

"He was doing all sorts of things for the city. He arranged the parade, ran the holiday raffle, and organized Christmas sales with the merchants downtown... It was all supposed to be a big shot in the arm for Charity. He was going to turn us into some sort of Christmas City U.S.A."

"That's why he was here? He was a Christmas consultant?"

"From what I understand. I'm going to have to speak to Harlan tomorrow and get more details."

"Pudding!"

Charlotte turned and spotted Aggie Mae Davis in a shiny purple robe with gold trim, her arms outstretched as she waddled toward the now frenzied terrier. The dog's barking increased until Aggie Mae unclipped it from the leash tethering it to the lamppost. Pudding wriggled into her waiting arms, all once again set right with his world.

Charlotte turned back to Frank. "I meant to ask, what was Pudding doing out there?"

Frank scratched at his cheek. "That's another thing. Damn dog was tied out front when the fire trucks got here. Nothing about this whole mess makes much sense."

"Someone choked a man dressed like a gingerbread man with an elf, tried to set his tree ablaze, and then tied a missing dog to the post in his front yard on the way out?"

"Near as I can tell."

"Totally weird." She couldn't help but take a moment to re-appreciate Frank's robe and gun look. "Though not half as weird as that getup you've got on."

Frank glanced down and then fought a failing battle to hide his own amusement. He tucked the robe a little tighter around his chest. "Help me out with this one, Charlotte. Is it the Internet?"

"Is *what* the Internet?"

Frank raised his hands, palms pointed to the ceiling. "Everything weird has something to do with the Internet. Did Kris meet someone on that Greg's Place? Is the costume some sort of kinky sex thing?"

Charlotte laughed. "*Craig's* List. Does Kris even have a computer?"

Frank nodded. "Yes. It's been bagged."

"So the techs will find things on that if they exist, right?"

Frank huffed. "I dunno. I don't know anything anymore. People dressing up like cookies—" He devolved into muttering.

"And no one saw anything?"

"No one's come forward. It's late. Everyone was in bed, but I have doofus out there asking around and doing door-to-doors."

"How'd you get the call about the body?"

"The fire. A neighbor smelled smoke and thought they saw a glow in here. They called the fire department, and the CFD called us. According to the fire guys, the dog was already outside barking. You can thank me that we have any evidence left at all. I got here just in time to keep the fire guys from blasting all the evidence down the storm drains. You know how they like to overdo things, just to be safe."

"Hello?" Aggie Mae peered through the screened porch door and into the house. "Charlotte? Is that you?"

"Hi, Aggie Mae."

Charlotte walked to the screened front porch, where Aggie Mae promptly threw her arms around her, pushing the dog tucked against her chest so tightly between her enormous breasts that Charlotte worried Pudding might suffocate.

"You found him," whispered Aggie Mae in her ear.

Charlotte couldn't help but smile. No matter how many murders she solved, she doubted anything could feel as good as returning a beloved pet to its owner, even if she didn't deserve credit.

"See? I told you not to worry."

Aggie Mae rocked Charlotte side-to-side until Charlotte realized she was trying to maneuver a better view inside Kristopher's house.

"Whatcha got goin' on in there?" Aggie Mae asked as Charlotte pulled from her death grip.

"Little fire. Bit of a crime scene, though, so we need to get you and Pudding out of here."

"Crime scene? You sayin' someone robbed the place?"

"No, I don't think so." Charlotte heard Sheriff Frank shut the front door and stopped bobbing in her attempts to block Aggie Mae's view.

Aggie Mae pointed over Charlotte's shoulder. "Is that a giant gingerbread man in there? Sittin' in a chair?"

Charlotte put a hand on the woman's arm to ease her away from the house. "The important part is you have Pudding back, right?"

Aggie raised the dog to press his head against her violet lips, but her gaze never left the house.

"Sure...sure... Ain't that Kris Rudolph's house?"

Charlotte succeeded in guiding Aggie Mae away from the house. She spotted Deputy Daniel leaning against his patrol car, staring at his phone. She'd grown up with Daniel and also knew him as the deputy her pawnshop-owner boyfriend, Declan, paid to let him know about deaths in the area. As unfortunate as it was, most of Declan's inventory came from the deceased, and it helped to know when people died.

"Daniel, can I talk to you?"

She patted Aggie Mae on the back to keep her moving into

the crowd and walked to the officer.

"This crowd's getting a little thick, don't you think?" she asked.

Daniel glanced around him and then back to Charlotte, his eyes as empty and unassuming as a bovine's.

She tried again. "I'm saying you should back them up or try to disperse them. Don't you think?"

Daniel scowled. "Why? They aren't hurting anybody."

"But they're too close. If one of them sees a little piece of the picture, and then another one spots another piece—by the time all the stories are swapped around in the pool tomorrow, they might have a pretty good view of the whole painting."

Daniel's brow knit. "What painting?"

Charlotte sighed. Aggie Mae and Kris's immediate neighbors already knew too much. Soon the machine would lurch into action. People would call friends who knew friends in the fire department and emergency services to find out more. By the next morning, all of Pineapple Port would know what happened. Or, at least, they'd think they did. *Not* knowing the full story never stopped anyone from sharing it.

"Our potential witnesses' memories will be compromised if people start sharing what *they* saw through the windows. Not to mention, sometimes, the best way to catch a bad guy is to withhold details of a crime from the press and the public. If a suspect lets slip, something only the real killer could know—" She paused. "Do you get where I'm going with this, Daniel?"

A smile curled the right side of the Deputy's mouth. "You must have watched a lot of detective shows when you were little to know all this stuff."

Charlotte sighed. She was in the middle of rephrasing her concerns when Frank's voice erupted behind her at full volume.

"Sweet baby peas, Daniel. She's telling you you need to get rid of these people *now. Can you hear me?*"

Startled, Daniel fumbled his phone into the air. It danced on his fingertips until he managed to snatch it and shove it into his pocket.

"Yes, sir. Gotcha."

Daniel ran around the other side of his vehicle to flip the sirens on and off. The crowd lurched in time with the burst of noise and then fell silent as Daniel held up his arms and addressed the crowd.

"I need all of you to go home now..."

Frank dropped his head into his hands and peeked up at Charlotte. "He could have killed half the neighborhood flipping on the siren like that."

Charlotte giggled.

Frank dropped his hands and stretched his back. "So you're going to help me with this case?"

She nodded. "Of course I will. I don't have anyone paying me to do anything else at the moment—"

"I'll pay you."

She gasped. "What? *Really*?"

"I'll make it official. I didn't expect you to work for free. I'll deputize you."

"*What*?" Charlotte's volume increased, and she bounced on her toes. She hadn't been this excited since Mariska bought her a ten-speed bike for Christmas as a kid. "You're going to make me a deputy?"

Frank waggled a finger at her. "Just for this case."

"Will I get a badge?"

"Sure. I'll give you a badge."

"Will I get a hat? The uniform's not particularly attractive, but I'll take a hat."

Frank cocked a hip, sending his shiny robe swaying. "You're saying this uniform isn't attractive?"

Charlotte laughed. "Okay, you got me. *That* outfit is gorgeous. I mean, the usual uniforms don't do much for me."

"Oh. Well, you still don't get a hat."

She pouted. "Shoot. You're no fun."

Frank shrugged. "Fine. I'll keep the badge..."

"No, I'm good. No hat, but I still get the badge. Deal?"

"Deal."

"*Deal*. Will I outrank Daniel?"

They turned and looked at the deputy, who had fallen into an argument with one of the local ladies about exactly how close she could stand to the house and still be far enough away.

Frank sighed. "Definitely."

CHAPTER FOUR

"Whatcha doing?" Darla wandered up Mariska's driveway with Turbo, her miniature Dachshund, in tow. The dog strained at the end of his leash, running circles around her.

Mariska looked up from her place on her knees. Her flashlight pointed through the crawlspace grate beneath her house. She wiped her brow and watched the dog gallop around Darla.

"You look like the Earth, with Turbo a little hot dog moon circling you."

Darla frowned. "Thanks for mentioning that. I just finished a huge piece of leftover lasagna, and I *feel* like a planet. What are you doing on your knees?"

"I'm looking for Scratchy."

"Scratchy?"

"He's a possum. I think."

"Ah. And he told you his name was Scratchy?"

"No, but he's under the house scratching around all night when I'm trying to get to sleep, so that's what I named him."

Darla nodded. "Makes sense."

"I'm going to put some poison out for him."

"You don't want to do that."

"Why not? He's just a giant rat. Maybe uglier than a rat."

"If you poison him, he'll die under there, and your whole house will smell to high heaven."

Mariska sat back on her heels. "I never thought of that."

"You need to hire a trapper."

"There's no money in the budget for critter trappers. We just had the roof replaced. And with Bob's ears, he doesn't hear a darn thing, so he doesn't care. If I told him I wanted to spend money catching a possum, he'd lose his mind."

Darla pointed at her. "Ooh, you know who had a possum? Layla. Her husband bought a trap. I bet she'd let us borrow it."

"What am I going to do with a possum if I trap it?"

"We'll take it somewhere and let it go."

Mariska struggled to get to her feet, and Darla moved forward to help. Once on her feet, Mariska put her hands on her hips and stared at the grate.

"Fine. I'll try and trap it if you promise to help."

"I'll help. We'll put some food in the cage and catch him. Easy-peasy."

"Catch *her*."

"It's a girl?"

Mariska nodded. "I just decided. She sounds like a girl. What do possums eat?"

Charlotte walked up the driveway, and the women turned before Darla could answer.

"Hey, what are you ladies up to?" she asked.

"What do possums eat?" asked Mariska.

Charlotte pursed her lips. "I want to say fish for some reason. I think I saw it on some critter trapper show. Why? Did you get a pet possum?"

"Not on purpose," grumbled Mariska, turning off her flashlight.

"We'll Google it," said Darla. "Let's go inside. It's hot out here, and I smell bacon."

The three ladies went inside Mariska's house. Charlotte had a smile she couldn't seem to squelch on her lips, and she saw Mariska spot it.

"What's up with you, Missy? You look like you have a secret."

Charlotte grinned. "Can *you* keep a secret?"

"You know we can't," said Darla. "But tell us anyway."

Charlotte nodded. "Okay. You'll find out from Frank anyway."

Darla scoffed. "Frank doesn't tell me anything."

Mariska tapped Darla's arm. "Let her say what it is."

Charlotte clapped her hands together and then held them out to her sides. "Frank wants me to help with an investigation, and he *deputized* me."

Mariska gasped. "Oh, that's *wonderful*. What does that mean?"

"He made me a deputy. He says he's going to give me a *badge*. Can you believe it? It's like wild west stuff."

Darla slid a piece of bacon from Mariska's communal plate and waved it at Charlotte like a wand. "Doesn't the deputized posse usually end up dead in those movies?"

Charlotte froze, mid-happy dance. "Do they?" She shrugged and resumed shaking her hips. "You know what? I don't even care. Now I'm a licensed private detective *and* a deputy. I'm, like, practically a superhero."

"I know about fifteen women who would love to sew you a costume," said Darla.

"I want to see the badge," said Mariska.

"I have to go talk to Frank later today. He said he'd give it to me if I swung by his office."

Mariska slapped Darla's hand as she reached for another strip of bacon. "Make a plate. Stop eating the bacon like an animal."

Darla flashed puppy eyes. "Be kind to me. My husband

deputized another woman. He never deputized *me*."

Charlotte laughed. "Because you'd go mad with power."

Darla snatched another strip of bacon and dodged a swipe of Mariska's spatula. "It's true."

CHAPTER FIVE

"Your honor, I'd like to call Danielle Arneau to the stand."

Stephanie Moriarty turned to watch her witness rise from her seat. The girl with scraggly hair pulled at her shirt, though no amount of tugging would ever get it to cover her pierced navel. She stooped to retrieve a pack of cigarettes that fell from her purse and then straightened.

Stephanie smiled in the most soothing way she could muster.

Okay, Danielle. Just remember what we practiced.

The girl's gaze met her own and then shot away.

Oh no.

Stephanie felt the acid from her morning coffee rise in her throat.

Danielle's focus slid to the right, and she stared at the back of the opposing counsel's head. Her hand fluttered to her throat to tug at a large necklace there. It took Stephanie a moment to read between the girl's fingers.

Danielle. The necklace said *Danielle* in large, scripty gold letters.

Not exactly Tiffany's, but still, it took a lot of gold to spell *Danielle*—

She's come into some money.

Stephanie's eyes grew wide.

No, no, no...not again. She's not going to say what we practiced—

Stephanie spun to face the judge. "Wait."

The judge looked up from her papers. "Did you say *wait*, Ms. Moriarty?"

"Yes, I—"

Danielle was staring at her now, frozen in her tracks, her face the mask of guilt. Assistant District Attorney Jason Walsh turned to face them. His eyes were wide as if he were surprised, but the smirk on his lips...

He knows. He got to her. Son of a—

"Ms. Moriarty?"

Stephanie turned her eyes to the judge, but her mind remained on the girl.

What am I going to do?

Danielle was her star witness. Her testimony would free the dirt bag sitting to her left, of that she was certain. But she could tell by the smug look on the crooked Assistant D.A.'s face that he knew that, too. This was the third time Walsh had tampered with her witnesses, paying them, she suspected, to tell his version of the truth.

Stephanie's fingers curled into fists.

He's supposed to be the good guy. He's supposed to play by the book and make it easy for me to beat him...

She glanced at her client. He was staring at her, too, his expression made all the more angry by the tattoo on his face—a smattering of tribal art spilling down his left temple and cheek with the word "badass" woven into it.

These people. They couldn't make it harder to keep them out of jail if—

The judge cleared her throat. "Ms. Moriarty? My patience is running low."

Stephanie flashed Danielle a glare sharp enough to slice through flesh and then slapped on a smile to face the judge. "Your honor, I'd like to request a continuance."

"Why?"

Stephanie glanced at Jason. His glee had ratcheted up a notch. She felt her own smile crack.

I am going to kill you.

"Ms. Moriarty?"

"Huh? Oh. Sorry. Permission to approach the bench, your honor?"

Judge Carrillo heaved a great sigh and motioned for Stephanie to approach.

"Me, too, your honor," said Jason, standing.

Stephanie heard a low growl thrum in her throat.

He really doesn't know who he's messing with.

The two lawyers walked to the bench, the sharp click of Stephanie's six-hundred-dollar heels the only sound.

Judge Carrillo's gaze locked on Stephanie's shoes and then bobbed up to meet her eyes.

"Are those Louboutin's?"

Stephanie nodded. "Would you like them?"

The judge chuckled. "Funny. So, tell me all about your problems."

Jason made a motion to show he acquiesced to Stephanie. She smiled with a touch of snarl and turned back to the judge.

"Your honor, I have reason to believe my witness has been tampered with. Possibly even bribed."

Jason gasped and slapped his hand to his chest. "Your honor, this is nothing short of slander. Convincing your witness to tell the *truth* instead of the *lies* opposing counsel groomed her to tell isn't what I'd call *tampering*."

The judge scowled. "You're both making serious accusations. Does anyone have any proof?"

Jason shook his head. "Not at this time, your honor."

The judge swiveled her attention back to Stephanie. "And you? What makes you think your witness has been tampered with?"

"It's—a feeling, your honor."

"So you want me to grant you a continuance on a *feeling*?"

Stephanie winced. "Well, no, I—"

The judge flopped back in her chair. "Look, today's your lucky day. We're just about out of time. I thought maybe I could squeeze this in, but it's late, and I have somewhere to be. I'm going to wrap things up, but I expect you both to be here tomorrow, ready to finish with no excuses and no whining about tampering without proof. Do you understand me?"

Both lawyers nodded.

The judge banged her gavel. "Okay, everyone, we're going to wrap up for today. I'll see you here tomorrow."

Stephanie walked back to her side of the room. Danielle saw her coming, snatched her worn, fake leather purse from a bench, and scurried out of the courtroom.

"Should have bought a new purse," Stephanie called after her.

"You better get me off," growled her client, standing as the police re-cuffed him to be returned to prison.

Stephanie rolled her eyes. "Have you considered getting a hate crime tattooed on your face? That would make it even *easier* for me."

The man's eyes narrowed, and he leaned forward, straining against the pull of the guard leading him toward the door. "The boss ain't gonna be happy with you if you don't set me free, you—"

The officer jerked him back as a string of profanities spilled from his lips.

Stephanie ignored him and stuffed her papers into her Italian leather briefcase.

"You seem a little flustered by your own client."

Stephanie turned to find Jason grinning at her.

She snorted a laugh. "Him? Growing up, my stepmother said worse things to me before breakfast on a daily basis. He's an *amateur*."

"Wow. That goes far towards explaining your charming demeanor."

Stephanie zipped her case shut and dropped it to her side. "You tampered with my witness."

Jason thrust his hands into his pockets and rocked on his heels. "Me? Why would I do that?"

"You're paying them—or threatening them—to lie because it's the only way you can beat me."

Jason scoffed. "Have you looked at your client? I don't have to pay anyone to put that punk in jail."

Stephanie smiled. "Remember the Wyatt case? Maybe not. I know it might be hard for you to recall *because you lost*. I'm sure all those losses blur together after a while."

"Sure. I remember Wyatt. I keep a list of all the killers and thieves you put back on the street right here." He tapped his skull with his index finger.

"Then it might interest you to know that after the Wyatt case, I went to talk to Wendy Brice—the witness who nearly blew the whole thing for me. Know what? She was *gone*. Seems she'd lucked into enough money to take herself and her three kids to Texas to live with her mother while she entered an expensive rehab."

Jason grinned. "Aw. That's a sweet story. Thank you for sharing it with me."

She poked him in the chest with her index finger. "I know you arranged it. I know you paid her to throw my client under the bus. You and your rich family. You're buying wins on your way to buying district attorney. Then maybe you can end up a senator like your daddy."

Jason shook his head. "Nope. Nice try, though."

Stephanie put her face an inch from his. "You don't want to mess with me."

"Stop working for scumbags, and I won't."

"Everyone has the right to a fair trial."

Jason snorted again and took a step back. "Do they, though?"

He strode up the aisle and, with a last wave, left the courtroom.

Stephanie frowned. She still had a few tricks up her sleeve to get this particular idiot out of his conviction, but this pattern had to end. Jason was making it more and more difficult for her to collect her checks. And the money wasn't even the most important part—the men she worked for didn't appreciate failure.

What she really needed was to take care of Jason once and for all. He couldn't disappear—he and his family were much too high-profile for such a simple solution. She needed to catch him in the act. Surely, he couldn't risk letting other people do his dirty work. He had to be paying these witnesses himself.

Maybe she could squeeze a few more bucks out of her client for a private investigator. Someone cheap. Someone honest and sweet who wouldn't be afraid of an Assistant D.A. because they couldn't fathom ever being arrested and up against him in court—

Stephanie slowed as she swung her bag onto her shoulder.

She smiled.

Charlotte.

Her ex's squeaky-clean new girlfriend was a shiny-new private investigator now.

She'd be perfect.

And as a bonus, any time Charlotte spent following Jason was time Declan would be left unattended.

CHAPTER SIX

Declan knocked on the door of the Pineapple Port modular home, and it rattled on its hinges. Crime tape still clung to the vinyl siding, flapping in the breeze.

He glanced left and right, wondering what eyes might be on him. He felt a little bad. When Charlotte told him the owner of 67 Hibiscus Dr. had died, his first thought had been, *"I wonder if he has any good bedroom furniture."*

The Hock o'Bell needed bedroom furniture.

Of course, he couldn't feel *too* bad about it. It *was* his job. And, after all, that's how Charlotte and he had met. Upon hearing a body had been found at *her* house, he'd shown up, hoping to be the first to approach the family about worldly goods left behind.

Funerals were expensive; sometimes, selling an unwanted desk or bookshelf was a great way to fund a burial.

In Charlotte's case, the "death" had turned out to be bones buried in her backyard garden, and Charlotte, the lovely occupant, remained very much alive.

He'd been wondering who to contact about the contents of Kristopher Rudolph's house when the man's wife called looking to sell out. He'd driven right over.

Declan raised his hand to knock again, only to have the door fling away from his reach. A thin woman with frizzy, dishwater-brown, and gray hair peered back at him. She looked as if a tornado had tossed her around for a few minutes and then dumped her back in the house.

She wiped her brow. "Yes?"

"Oh. Hello there." Declan flashed her his best smile, the one that made the dimple near his right cheek deepen. He knew immediately his effort had been wasted. The woman stared, unmoving. He'd have received the same reaction flashing his dimple at a telephone pole.

Okay, so the charming pawnbroker act isn't going to win over this one.

Declan cleared his throat and fumbled for the card he'd thrust in his pocket back at the shop.

"I'm Declan Bingham. I own the pawn shop in town, the Hock o' Bell. You called me? I—"

The woman closed her eyes and took a deep breath as he spoke and then cut him short without reopening them. "And you were hoping to vulture up some stuff. I'm Noelle. Come on in."

He frowned. He hated the word *vulture*.

Noelle took a step back, and Declan entered the home without comment. He'd been called a vulture before. He tried to take it in stride. By the end of every visit, the widows and widowers were tearfully grateful to him for helping them unload their excess furniture at such fair prices.

He knew the drill. No pressure. He could always come back later. Mrs. Rudolph would soon come to see he wasn't a vulture—

Declan stopped in his tracks, the riot of color and clutter in the house sending his mind into overload. Charlotte hadn't been kidding when she described the house to him.

Take a deep breath.

He kept his own house military-neat, or at least as neat as he could with his slob of an uncle, Seamus, still crashing there. It had been nearly six months since Seamus showed up. He knew because he kept a prison-wall-like calendar next to his bed where he scratched out the days he'd been forced to share a roof with the man.

Kristopher Rudolph's home looked like the day after a black Friday sale at a Christmas-themed dollar store. Decorations dotted the landscape like red poppies in a field of green. The furniture had been pulled away from the walls, the Christmas tree was burned, and every pot, pan, and plate had been yanked from the kitchen cabinets and now sat teetering in piles on the counters and floor.

"Wha—?" began Declan, realizing the answer to his question before he'd posed it. His attention had circled back to settle on the woman, and for the first time, he noticed a glistening sheen of sweat on her face and neck. Unless she'd been enjoying a workout tape in one of the back rooms, she was clearly responsible for creating the mess.

She'd been looking for something. Declan couldn't help but wonder if she'd found it.

"How much ya give me?" She held a steady gaze on him as if daring him to ask what had happened. She flopped into a large reclining chair, and he eyeballed the La-Z-Boy's burned arm.

Too bad. La-Z-Boys were good sellers.

He'd heard there'd been a fire, but sniffing the air, it didn't seem as though everything had been ruined by smoke. Maybe in the living room but not the back rooms. It appeared the fire had been contained to the area around the Christmas tree, which, unfortunately, included the chair.

"How much for what? What do you want to sell?" he asked, trying to seem unenthusiastic. It wasn't hard.

She made a lasso-twirling-like motion in the air with her hand. "Everything."

"The furniture?"

"*Everything.* This." She picked up a ceramic angel and held it aloft. "This." She put down the angel and tossed a piece of shriveled tinsel into the air without fanfare.

He watched the tinsel float to the ground. "Uh, can I look around?"

Nodding, she stood and smacked a cigarette from a pack which seemed to have magically manifested in her hand.

"I'll be outside." She glanced at the pile of ash beneath the tree. "Not that it matters."

He bobbed to the right as she passed to keep her from clipping his shoulder.

Charming woman.

Declan took a deep breath and surveyed the room, making a mental list.

Coffee table and chair, toast. Lamp, nope. The other table... could maybe be refinished. Flat-screen television, potentially salvageable. Few usable decorations and knickknacks...

He strode into the kitchen and opened the few cabinets not already hanging open.

Nothing worth anything unless she includes the appliances...

Down the hall, he peered into an almost empty office. The contents of a three-tier file cabinet had been tossed to the floor.

Desk. Chair. File cabinet.

On to the master bedroom.

Decent headboard. Decent side table. What the...

Declan took a step back to better survey the strangest bureau he'd ever laid eyes on—and that was saying something in his business. The piece had thirty-one drawers of varying sizes, each with a flat, brightly-painted wooden knob shaped like a different creature, object, or Christmas icon. A rabbit, giraffe, dog, tree, ornament, cat, raccoon...the last drawer featured a pineapple. Half the drawers were open. Most were empty. Underwear had been stuffed into the horse drawer, and socks in the robin.

Declan stroked his chin. "Now *that* is unique."

He made his way back outside to find the woman stamping out her smoke in the grass.

He cleared his throat. "I'm sorry, was it Noelle?"

She nodded.

"And you're Kris's—?

"Wife. *Ex*-wife. I got everything in the will. They contacted me."

"Okay. You wouldn't happen to have any proof that you have the right to sell his things?"

"I have everything signed and official." Rolling her eyes, Noelle turned and walked to a faded red Chevy Malibu to open the passenger side door. Papers slid from the seat to the curb as she shuffled through them. She made no attempt to retrieve the ones that fell. When Noelle found what she was looking for, she slammed shut the door, catching papers half in and half out. Turning, she marched her proof back to Declan.

"You can keep them if you need to. I have copies."

He couldn't keep his gaze from bouncing back to the pile of papers laying in a puddle beside the Malibu.

She had copies of *everything*, apparently.

He looked over the will, and it seemed legit. All of Kris's worldly goods were earmarked for Noelle. What he assumed was Kris's mess of a signature, Noelle's signature, and the mark of the lawyer graced the bottom.

"So how much?" she asked.

He scratched his head. "There isn't much in there. Would you take...four hundred?"

"Five."

"Including appliances?"

"It's a rental. Those aren't his."

"But everything else is?"

"Yep."

He did the math. He felt pretty confident he could get close to five hundred for the unique chest of drawers alone.

"Fine. Deal."

"You got it on ya?"

Declan reached for his wallet. He always brought cash in the hopes the sight of it would move a reluctant seller to sell.

He'd barely pulled the bills from his wallet when she snatched them from his hand.

"Great. Here you go." She reached into her pocket and tossed him a set of house keys on a Christmas tree ring. "Place has to be cleaned out by Thursday."

She turned and headed for her car.

Declan followed her. "Wait—I don't want *everything*."

"You just bought everything."

"I'm not a junkman."

She opened her door. "Could've fooled me."

Declan scowled. "Do you have a number in case I have any questions?"

Her wry smile proved her first and last sign of emotion.

"I'm going back to Wisconsin. He's your problem now."

CHAPTER SEVEN

Charlotte tugged Abby's leash and slowed as she approached Kristopher Rudolph's home. The dog looked up at her, annoyed to have her walk interrupted.

Abby didn't scowl at her mother for long. Declan appeared on Kristopher's doorstep and her moppy head whipped in his direction, her nub of a tail spinning like a propeller. Charlotte leaned down and unclipped the dog's leash so the eager Wheaton could tear off and say hello.

"Hey, how are you doing today, Princess Fuzzball?" Declan leaned down to scratch Abby beneath her ears and kiss her nose. Greetings over, Abby got to business and pushed past him to let herself inside Kris Rudolph's house to explore.

"Here you are, picking the carcass. You're such a *vulture*," said Charlotte, knowing how much the term bothered him.

He held up his palms and shook them. "Oh, excuse me. You're a *big* deputy now, making fun of the little people who knew you *when*."

She grinned. She'd confessed to being deputized on the phone with Declan the night before, about two seconds after it happened. "It's true. But while we're on the topic, how did you end up at my crime scene?"

"Crime scene?"

Whoops. Frank had told her not to let anyone know Kris was murdered yet. She hated not to tell Declan, though...maybe she could just delay it a bit longer and get the go-ahead from Frank soon.

She backtracked. "I mean, someone *died* here. Doesn't mean it was a *crime*."

"Uh huh." Declan noticed a tiny, torn piece of crime tape and flicked it as he stepped down off the porch and walked to her. "Looks like they removed the tape. It's not a crime scene anymore."

She put a hand on her hip, realizing she hadn't heard the techs were finished their work. "I have to admit, not knowing the crime tape came down makes me feel a little less deputy-ish."

Declan slid his hands down her arms and pecked her on the lips.

"That's an official cop term? Deputy-ish?"

She snickered and looked away, embarrassed by how his attentions made her heart flutter. "Yes. You wouldn't know it, being a *commoner* and all."

"I'm pretty sure not being a deputy makes me a *civilian*, not a commoner."

She shrugged. "Potato, potahto."

He took a step back and assumed a supercilious countenance. "Well, Ms. Deputy, you can forget your *vulture* stuff. I didn't come creeping. She called *me*."

"She?"

"The wife."

Charlotte perked. Kris's wife could be *full* of important information. "Is she here?"

He shook his head. "She's long gone. Stuck me with the whole house. Trash and treasure. Mostly trash."

"Long gone? Where?"

"Said she was going back to Wisconsin."

"Back to *Wisconsin*? She must have swept into town, called you, and left."

"Not before she tore the house apart."

"It's a mess?"

He nodded.

Charlotte sighed. "I'm sure Frank would have liked to talk to her. I know I would have."

"Sorry. It didn't hit me until she was driving off that maybe I should have called you a little sooner. I didn't expect her to leave like that."

"What was her name?"

"Noelle."

Charlotte cocked an eyebrow. "You're kidding."

"It's spelled differently if that helps."

"Oh, that makes all the difference in the *world*. How is it possible he married a Noelle?"

Declan shrugged, smirking. "That's what she told me. It's how she signed the papers she gave me, too."

He pulled a set of folded papers from his pocket and handed them to Charlotte.

"Kris left everything he owns to Noelle *Kringle*," she read aloud. She looked up at him. "This keeps getting weirder and weirder." She scrutinized Kris's signature, but it was nothing more than a scribble—impossible to read.

Abby appeared on the screened porch, tongue hanging out. She checked to be sure Charlotte hadn't left and then bolted off again to inspect the rest of the house.

Charlotte headed for the door. "Can you tell if Noelle took anything?"

He shook his head and fell into line behind her. "Her car was full of papers and mountains of junk, but I don't know if she arrived that way or not."

Charlotte crossed the porch and entered the open door of the home. All the decorations she remembered gawking at the night of the murder had been moved, tipped over, or otherwise misplaced. The kitchen looked as if a poltergeist had run through it.

"The place is a disaster. She did all this?"

Declan shrugged. "I assume so. She was sweaty and frazzled when I showed up. She'd been doing *something*. I guess it didn't look like this when you were here before?"

"No. I mean, the ash was there, but other than that, it looked like a normal house in a normal state of disarray. If you can call owning every Christmas decoration on the planet normal."

Charlotte strolled through the room and as far into the kitchen as she could without tripping on the utensils scattered about the floor.

"She was looking for something."

"Seems like it."

"Do you feel like she found it? Did she seem... *satisfied*?"

Declan tilted his head as if considering her question. "No. Now that you mention it, she seemed miserable."

"Mad?"

"More...defeated."

"Hm. Maybe what she's looking for is still here."

"Or maybe he kept what she wanted in another spot. A storage unit or something."

Charlotte pointed at Declan. "Good call. I'll have Frank look into that."

"You should look fast. If all those papers in her car came from Kris's house, she might find a receipt for a storage unit among them. Could be why she took them all."

Charlotte grimaced. "Another good point."

Declan patted her on the shoulder. "I wouldn't worry too much. If she found a receipt for a storage unit, she didn't let on. She didn't seem *hopeful*. I believed her when she said she was heading to Wisconsin. Her last words were, *He's your problem now.*"

"Oh my. Bitter, much?"

"Bitter's a good word. It was almost as if he'd pulled

something over on her one last time."

"Yikes."

Declan shrugged. "I could be reading too much into it. Could be she's just not a very jolly person."

"Ironically."

Charlotte peered down the hall, searching for Abby. She spotted the dog's butt sticking out from the doorway.

"Abby. Let's go."

The Wheaten ignored her, which wasn't unusual.

Charlotte walked down the hall and playfully smacked the dog's furry tush. Abby barely moved, her nose pressed to the floor behind the open door. Charlotte could hear her snorfing like a furry pig.

She stuck her head in the bathroom and, searching for the object of Abby's fascination, closed the door against her chest to look behind it. Shallow grooves marred the bottom of the door as if a small dog had tried to dig his way through.

"He had Pudding in here," she said. "I missed this the other night."

"What's that?" asked Declan, appearing at the end of the hall.

"When I got here the night Kris died, Aggie Mae's missing dog, Pudding, was tied to the lamppost out front."

"Didn't she hire you to find that dog?"

"I wouldn't say *hired*. I wasn't going to charge her for looking for her dog. But yes, he was missing. I thought Pudding had been nearby when everyone showed up for the fire, and someone tethered him to keep him safe."

"But now you don't think so?"

"There are scratch marks back here." She pushed Abby out of the way so Declan could poke in his head to see. "Someone had a dog locked in here."

"Why would he have stolen Aggie Mae's dog?"

"Maybe he found it? Maybe he planned to take him to her in

the morning?"

Declan chuckled. "But if he stole it, Aggie Mae's a suspect now."

Charlotte laughed. "She wouldn't have killed him. She'd could probably put a dent in him, though."

She took a deep breath and expelled it slowly.

"But..." Declan prompted. She looked at him and realized he could tell she'd had a thought.

"If he *had* found Pudding, who tied the dog out front? He was dead in his chair."

"Maybe he tied it there to let it go to the bathroom."

"Maybe..."

Charlotte walked to the front door. She stared through the screens at the lamppost and then wandered back into the house.

Her gaze settled on what was left of the ash pile. The crime technicians had taken most of the ash to pick through it in the hopes a bit of evidence might be found.

Declan reappeared in the living room with Abby in his arms.

"Forget something?"

"I wasn't leaving. I was looking at the post outside. Then I remembered that." She pointed at the ash.

"What about it?"

Charlotte picked her words carefully. As far as the world knew, the Santa impersonator died the same night a small fire broke out in his home. There was no murder. No choking-by-elf. She hated not sharing the information with Declan, but she also didn't want to blow her first week as a deputy.

"This fire might have been deliberately set," she mumbled.

"What makes you say that?"

"If it was, it could be someone put the dog outside where he would be safe."

"Hm." Declan set Abby down next to Charlotte, and she clipped on the dog's leash. "All I know is I bought this mess. I need to finish picking through things. Blade should be here soon with the truck to help me tote the big stuff."

They walked outside and chatted about plans for dinner until Charlotte felt a shadow fall across her skin. It felt as though something large had eclipsed the sun.

"Afternoon, Miss Charlotte."

Charlotte bent back her neck to peer up at Blade, Declan's top salesperson and the largest man she'd ever seen. Blade looked like a monster Viking sent through time and space to work at a pawn shop. Though he could crush her head in his dinner-plate-sized paws, she never feared the gentle giant. Blade insisted he'd been christened with his threatening name by his mother, a hippie, who likened him to a blade of grass. His propensity for wearing t-shirts featuring various types and brands of weapons made her wonder, though.

"Hey Blade, nice to see you. Here to pick up Declan's ill-gotten gains?"

"They weren't *ill-gotten*. I paid five hundred dollars for it all," muttered Declan.

"Five hundred? Was it worth that?"

He nodded. "There's some pretty interesting furniture in the master bedroom. The chest of drawers alone is huge and unique."

She nodded. "I saw that. Seemed like something old 'Christmas Kris's would own."

She started towards the sidewalk. "I'll get out of your way and go let Frank know Noelle was here. He's going to be mad he missed her. If she's as disgruntled as you described, she could be a suspect."

Declan's eyes grew wide. "Wait. You're saying Kris was murdered?"

She put her hand over her mouth. "I didn't say that."

He chuckled. "Maybe wait an hour before you tell Frank. Let us get this stuff out of here. I don't need him stopping me, thinking everything has to be searched again since her visit."

Charlotte scowled and put her hand on her hip. "Mr.

Bingham, are you trying to stand in the progress of police work?"

He pinched his forefinger and thumb together. "Maybe a little."

She chuckled. "Fine. He knows where to find you if he needs you."

CHAPTER EIGHT

Charlotte walked Abby home, lost in thought about the possibility that someone had started the fire in Kris's home. She glanced up as she turned the corner onto her street and spotted a red Viper parked in her driveway. A blonde stood on her porch, staring at her, her fist raised in mid-knock.

Stephanie.

Charlotte quickened her step as Stephanie awaited her arrival, hands on hips.

"There you are," said Stephanie. Her tone implied it had been rude of Charlotte to not be home.

Charlotte's eyes squinted.

Any time Declan's ex showed up, things took a turn for the worse.

She walked up the slight incline of her driveway, Abby tugging on her leash, eager to greet her visitor.

Apparently, dogs can't smell evil.

From the top of the small landing, Stephanie peered down at the dog, her lip curled.

"Keep the mutt away from me."

"You're standing in front of *her* door."

Charlotte pulled Abby back far enough for Stephanie to walk

down the three stairs in her four-inch red heels. She didn't even wobble. Charlotte couldn't help but think that if she tried to navigate the stairs in those heels, she would end up sprawled in the driveway.

"I'll put her inside." Charlotte opened the front door and pushed Abby inside before closing the door. She turned and peered down at Stephanie, enjoying being in the position of power, even if it were by only three feet.

"To what do I owe the pleasure of you darkening my door?"

Stephanie smiled. To Charlotte, Stephanie's smile always appeared a little like a snake eyeing up a baby bird for lunch. She hated feeling like the baby bird.

Stephanie flicked her hair from her eyes. "I have a job for you."

Charlotte laughed. "You've got to be kidding. I wouldn't work for you if you gave me ten thousand dollars and a lemon meringue pie."

Stephanie cocked an eyebrow, but Charlotte refused to explain the bit about the pie. She knew it was an odd thing to mention, but she'd been thinking about lemon meringue pie during the walk home and hadn't quite gotten over the idea.

Stephanie let it pass. "I think you *will* work for me."

"Why's that?"

"Because if you do, I'll give you my mother's ledger."

Charlotte frowned. "I don't know what that means."

"The ledger she kept of all her local clients. Her *protected* clients."

Charlotte's lips slipped open a crack. Stephanie's mother, Jamie Moriarty, had worked for the witness protection program. Either due to laziness or to amuse herself, she'd assigned many of her 'clients'—many of them criminals who had ratted out their bosses to avoid jail—new lives in Charity. Every time a crime occurred in the area, Charlotte couldn't help but wonder if the perpetrator was one of Jamie Moriarty's clients, reliving his or her glory days.

Charlotte tried to erase any expression of eagerness from her face. The last thing she wanted Stephanie to know was how much she'd *love* to have that list. "Just because they're in witness protection, it doesn't mean they're flipped criminals."

Stephanie laughed. "Oh, hers were. I promise you that."

Charlotte took a deep breath and relaxed her shoulders.

Cool. Be cool.

"How could she even have a ledger? It would be incredibly dangerous to keep all those new identities in a book. Your mother's not that stupid."

"There's only very specific information."

"What does that mean?"

Stephanie leaned into her car and pulled out a leather-bound book. She opened it for Charlotte to see and flipped through a few of the pages. Each page contained a giant swirly design.

"Fingerprints?"

Stephanie nodded. "That's all there is."

"What good is that to me?"

"Whenever there's a crime in town, wouldn't it be nice to know if you're up against a loose-lipped hitman from New York City or a local idiot?"

Charlotte scowled. "In theory. So we could see if any prints found at the scene matched any of the prints in that book?"

"Kind of."

"What do you mean, kind of?"

"Well, all these prints have been expunged from the system."

Charlotte nodded. "So if we find prints and they don't exist in the system, instead of assuming we're working with a first-time criminal, we can compare them to your book and know if we're dealing with a nobody or a *somebody*."

"Exactly."

"That doesn't tell us *which* somebody, though."

"No. But once you know this much, who knows—combined with other clues—you might have all you need to put the pieces together. It will at least let you know if you need to be worried or *really* worried."

Charlotte sighed and leaned back against her door. "What is it you want me to do in exchange for this possibly useless, possibly slightly helpful book of magic?"

Stephanie grinned. "It's super simple. I need you to follow Jason Walsh over the weekend."

"Who's Jason Walsh? Another man who figured out you're a psycho and tried to run? Can I give him a head start?"

Stephanie scowled. "He's an assistant district attorney."

"This sounds illegal."

"It's not. I'm the good guy this time. He's cheating to make me lose a case. He's a spoiled rich kid who thinks laws don't apply to him."

"But he works for the government. Your clients are all scumbags."

"They still deserve a *fair* trial."

Charlotte grunted. "I suppose. What do you think he's doing?"

"He's meddling. Paying my witnesses to flip sides. I have an important witness who's going to win this case for me on Monday. I have to reveal I'm using her as a witness on Friday. That gives him the weekend to pay her off and destroy my case. I need a third party—someone he wouldn't recognize—to keep an eye on him."

"Why me? There are other detectives."

"Sure. But why *not* you?"

"Because you hate me."

Stephanie pouted. "Aww. Why would you think that? Does it hurt your wittle heart?"

"Spare me. You're up to something."

"Yeah, I'm up to *hiring you*."

Charlotte sighed. "I dunno...it feels a little like a spider asking a fly to hop into her web."

"Look, I promise. I need a detective. You're a detective. And you're cheap."

Charlotte squinted. "Watch it."

"I have something you want. Something I don't need. It doesn't get any cheaper than that."

"I'll think about it. Expenses?"

"I'll throw in expenses."

Charlotte nodded as her gaze fell to the leather-bound book.

It would make a great Christmas present for Frank...

"Give me a minute to think about it. I'll call you."

Stephanie smiled. "Great. Declan has my number."

Charlotte felt her cheek twitch. "*I* have your number."

"Great." With the flash of another grin, Stephanie slid into her Viper and drove away with a squeal of wheels.

CHAPTER NINE

Charlotte took the rest of the day to finish her embroidery work and get all the gifts in the mail. She'd called Frank to let him know about Noelle, but Darla had talked him into an impromptu holiday shopping trip, and he'd taken the day off. Charlotte guessed he was too cranky to answer his phone.

She finished up a few loose ends the next morning and then crossed the street to borrow Mariska's car.

I really need to get a car.

Before becoming a private investigator, she'd had little reason to use a car. She worked from home and could walk to the food store. Now, she was having a hard time imagining pedaling around behind the Assistant D.A. on her ten-speed.

Mariska never minded her borrowing the Volkswagen, but then, that was when she borrowed it once a week to run an errand. Keeping it day after day for surveillance could be an inconvenience.

Mariska wasn't home, but Charlotte had a spare key. She looked at her watch and guessed Mariska had gone to the pool. She wouldn't need the car for a little while.

She drove the VW to the Sheriff's office, still mulling Stephanie's offer as she walked in through the front door.

A goldfish swam circles in a bowl on the counter as Linda, the new receptionist, stopped her paper shuffling.

"He's in," she said. She knew Charlotte sometimes stopped by to see Frank.

Charlotte smiled and held up a hand. "Thanks. How are you?"

Linda sighed. "Oh, you know. Never enough money and never enough time. And my nephew's gotten the neighbor girl pregnant."

Charlotte winced. "Yikes. Or congratulations..."

"You said it. I don't think anyone's decided which yet."

Charlotte took another step.

"Of course, the pregnancy takes my mind off the cancer."

Charlotte stopped. "What's that?"

"My father. Prostate cancer."

"I'm sorry to hear that."

"Apparently, they all get it at his age."

"So it isn't anything to worry about?"

She shrugged. "We don't know yet. With his luck, it'll probably kill him."

Charlotte remained frozen in place, afraid if she took another step, Linda's goldfish might float to the top of his bowl.

"Well...Hope everything works out okay, and you have a good Christmas."

Linda snorted. "*Christmas.* Don't even get me started."

Charlotte scurried down the hall and tapped lightly on Sheriff Frank's open office door. He looked up.

"What are you doing here, Deputy Morgan?"

Charlotte couldn't stop a grin from leaping to her lips. "You told me to stop by today to start on the Rudolph case."

"Oh, right. Come in. Shut the door."

She stepped in and closed his office door behind her.

"You made it past Suzy Sunshine." Frank jerked a thumb towards the front office.

"She's in rare form this morning."

Frank nodded. "By the time I got back here, I was about ready to hang myself. This morning she said the sprinkles on the donuts reminded her of all the pills her mother has to take."

Charlotte chuckled. "I'm afraid I have some more bad news for you."

"Uh oh. Last time somebody started a conversation like that, Darla'd driven the Ford into the pond."

"Compared to that, I guess my news isn't that bad. Or it's worse...depends."

"Spill it."

"Kris Rudolph has an ex-wife, Noelle Kringle."

"Noelle Kringle? You're kidding. She bring the kids, Jingle and Bells?"

"No kids that I know of."

"How'd you find this out?"

"She was at Rudolph's house yesterday. She sold all his furniture to Declan."

Frank straightened. "Is she still there?"

"No. That's the bad news. She tore the place apart, called Declan, sold him the stuff she hadn't destroyed, and headed back to Wisconsin."

"Wisconsin?"

"That's what she told Declan."

"Why didn't he stop her? Why didn't you tell me?"

"He didn't know she was important to the case. We haven't told anyone it was a murder yet, remember? And I tried to call you yesterday, but you didn't answer your phone."

"*Darla.*" Frank slapped the tips of his fingers on the edge of his desk. "Dang. I would have really liked to talk to her." He looked up at Charlotte. "What did you mean about her destroying things?"

"Drawers open, things strewn about...I think she was looking for something."

"What?"

She shrugged.

Frank dropped his hands into his lap and leaned back so far in his chair that Charlotte worried he'd flip it. "She give him any proof she had the right to sell his stuff?"

"Declan said she had a signed will. He's got a copy of it if you want it."

"She must have already identified the body. Why didn't Roger do me the courtesy of letting me know she—"

"Who's Roger?"

"Coroner. County has the body, and they've got people looking into things, but they're as dry as we are on this one so far."

"Still no leads?"

Frank lifted his hands in the air and snapped back to the upright position. "Worse than that. We hardly know a thing about Kristopher himself, let alone who killed him. Turns out that's not his real name. I doubt it's *Kringle* either."

Charlotte frowned, recalling Stephanie's fingerprint book. Could Kristopher be the victim of a revenge killing? Had he been a witness? She'd hoped to keep the book a secret until the holiday, but it seemed they might need it sooner than she'd thought. "I might be able to help you with his identity."

Frank perked. "Yeah? How so?"

"Stephanie has a book of fingerprints."

"Stephanie—Declan's ex-girlfriend?" He swirled his finger against the side of his head to demonstrate he considered the woman one or two eggs short of an omelet.

Charlotte nodded. "That one."

"What's a book of fingerprints? And since when are you and Stephanie bosom buddies?"

"Good question. I'm still trying to work out that bit myself. She's offered me a book containing the fingerprints of all the criminals her mother had stashed in witness protection—*here,* in

Charity."

"You think Kristopher could have been killed for what he saw or said?"

"Maybe. It might explain why this all seems so odd."

"Where's this book?"

"I don't have it yet. Actually, I was going to give it to you for Christmas."

Frank clapped his hands together. "Christmas is coming early this year. I need it now."

"I haven't done the work she hired me to do yet."

"In exchange for the book?"

She nodded. "She thinks an assistant district attorney is tampering with her cases. She wants proof. Wants me to follow him for the weekend."

Frank sighed and rubbed his hand across the top of his head. "Can you get the book early?"

"I can try. Can you get me Kris's fingerprints? If she won't get me the whole book, maybe she'll at least let me see if his prints match any of them. Sort of a test run."

"I can do that. We've really only got one or two leads so far, but they're not great."

"Who?"

"Jimmy the Jeweler called me this morning wanting to know if we found any rings at Kris's. Seems he lent one to him."

"If there were rings there, I imagine Noelle has them now."

"That's what I'm afraid of. We weren't looking for rings when we did our sweep. I was going to go back this afternoon, but it seems I'm too late."

"What did he lose? I'll ask Declan to keep an eye out."

"A ruby-emerald ring."

"How Christmassy."

"That was the idea. It was for the Christmas raffle. Kris was going to put it on display during the parade, but Jimmy says he didn't see it anywhere, and when he tried to find out why, Kris avoided him."

"Kris was *dead* by the end of the day. Does that count as *avoiding* someone?"

Frank shrugged. "I believe Jimmy believes something wasn't right."

Charlotte wandered across the room in thought. "Jimmy's angry about the missing ring, and the next thing you know, Kristopher is dead? Should we be worried about that?"

Frank scoffed. "Aw, Jimmy didn't kill anyone over a ring. The ex-wife probably had more reasons to kill him than Jimmy, but I'm going to have to track her down to find out if it's true."

"She did show up awfully quickly."

Frank nodded.

Charlotte sat in the chair across from Frank. "You said one or *two* leads. You have another?"

"The Mayor."

"The Mayor?"

"He's been acting really squirrelly. Haven't figured out why yet."

"How so?"

Frank shrugged. "He's been asking a lot of questions. Tell you what. Why don't you go and talk to Jimmy, and I'll talk to the Mayor."

Charlotte saluted. "Aye, aye, sir."

He rolled his eyes. "You're my deputy. Not in the navy."

"What do you guys say?"

"For you? Just *Sure, Uncle Frank* will do."

She grinned. "I've never called you *uncle*. You've always been *Frank*."

"Fine. Solve the crime, and you can call me whatever you want."

"Deal." She saluted again.

Frank chuckled. "Oh, and here." He opened a drawer and tossed something at her. Taken off guard, she bobbled the flat item until she'd grasped it. She held it in her palm and smiled.

"My very own badge."

"Your very own badge. Flash it with pride."

"Can I wear it?"

"On a tank top? No. Just keep it in your pocketbook in case you need it."

Charlotte pouted. "Fine. You're no fun."

Charlotte danced out of the room, repeatedly pretending to flash the badge. "Deputy Morgan here. I'm Deputy Morgan. That's Deputy Morgan to you, punk."

"That's very unprofessional," called Frank after her. "Hold on. I need to get you the printout of Kris's fingerprint."

Charlotte jogged back into the office and waited while Frank wrestled with his printer. When the ornery machine finished its work, he handed her the printout.

"Here."

Charlotte assumed an expression she hoped looked James-Bond-debonair. "Thank you. I'm Morgan. *Deputy* Morgan."

Frank rolled his eyes. "Get out of here, you loon."

CHAPTER TEN

Charlotte drove to Jimmy the Jewelers, eager to interview him as her first official job as a deputy. As elated as she was to have her badge, she felt a tickling dread teasing the back of her mind. She sat waiting for the light to change and realized the cause of her unease.

Stephanie.

She hated the idea of working for the bloodthirsty, sneaky wench, but the fingerprint book *could* be a handy thing to have. She parked near Jimmy's and looked down at the phone sitting in the passenger seat.

Might as well get this over with.

She reached for her phone and dialed.

Stephanie didn't bother to say hello.

"You know, if we were sister wives, I'd be the original wife, and you'd be the young new thing who seems exciting for a while, but it's always *me* Declan comes back to in the end."

Charlotte scowled at her phone and then raised it back to her ear. "Can't you just answer the phone with *hello* like a normal person?"

"Consider it my daily observation."

Here's an observation for you. You're a b—

"Decided you needed the fingerprints after all?" asked Stephanie.

Charlotte wanted to throw the phone out the window. Stephanie had known all along she'd come crawling back for the book and she *hated* proving her right.

"Yes. I'll follow the D.A. for you."

"*Assistant* D.A. Don't start giving that jerk a raise."

"Whatever. Do you have an address for him?"

"You're the detective. It's not like he invites me to dinner parties."

"Fine. Can I have the book now?"

"No, you can't have the book now. In what world does that make sense?"

"In what world does me following this man for a weekend and trusting *you* to then hand over the book make sense?"

"I'll give you half."

Charlotte considered the offer. While half sounded good, if Kristopher Rudolph wasn't in the half she received, she'd have no way of knowing if he were in the *other* half. That's all she really needed to know at the moment. "Tell you what. Right now, I really only need *one*."

"One fingerprint?"

"Right. A specific one. If it exists."

"Isn't half the book better than one print?"

"I'm looking for one particular print. If you give me half, and the one I need isn't in *that* half, then I'm stuck."

"Then you wait a few days."

"I don't want to wait a few days."

Stephanie sighed. "How do you propose we do this? I'm not going to sit here comparing your fingerprint to the book."

"I'll do it. I'll sit in your office and do it."

Stephanie went silent.

"Hello?" prompted Charlotte.

Stephanie's voice returned, and Charlotte could hear the she-devil's amusement the second she began to speak. "Tell you what. Send Declan over with the fingerprint, and he can search the book."

Charlotte closed her eyes. *She really never misses a trick.*

She resolved to make Stephanie state her reasoning for requesting Declan out loud. Maybe if she *heard* herself say something so pathetic—

"Why do you want Declan to do it? Are you afraid I'll memorize them?"

Stephanie laughed. "Right. Because I think you're a *genius.*"

"So you just want to be near Declan? Isn't that kind of...oh, I dunno...*sad*?"

"No. Just another example of how I can make him come to me any time I like."

Charlotte felt her temper rise and warned herself to keep her mouth shut. If she said what was on *her* mind, Stephanie would burn the book.

"Want to know what I tease him about when we're together?" asked Stephanie during the lull.

Charlotte took a deep, calming breath. "Not at all, thanks."

"His taste in women lately."

Charlotte rolled her eyes. "Ha. Ooh, got me there. Sizzle burn. I'll get back to you with a time Declan can swing by. Goodbye."

She hung up and pulled into a parking spot down the block from Jimmy the Jeweler. She had things to do, but first, she thought she'd sit and stew for a minute.

Why Stephanie thought Declan would ever want anything to do with her again, after everything she'd done—

Hm. Good point. What if he *refused* to go see Stephanie? She really needed the book. She'd be thrown into the awkward position of begging him to spend time with Stephanie.

Probably exactly what she'd wanted.

Someone knocked loudly on the hood of the car, and Charlotte jumped, yanked from her thoughts by what felt like a minor heart attack.

She looked out the window and spotted Declan's uncle Seamus waving at her, an enormous grin on his glistening face. Even his short gray hair appeared soaked with sweat.

She stepped out of her car.

"What are you doing here? You almost scared me to death," she said.

"Sorry, I saw you sittin' there and couldn't help myself." Seamus pulled a rag from the waistband of his shorts and used it to wipe his face as Charlotte stared at the building in front of them. She knew it as Chuck's—a dive bar she'd never actually stepped inside before. The place was in the paper every week for some sort of altercation—a fight outside, a fight inside, health department violations... The sign that used to hang over the bar had been pulled down and now leaned against the wall, the shadow of its shape still burned into the frontage.

"You're kind of sweaty for just leaving a bar. Some sort of new competitive drinking event?"

Seamus tucked the rag back into his belt. "I'm not leavin' the bar. I'm buyin' it. Well, *bought* it, truth be told."

"You bought Chuck's?"

"Aye. I'm in the process of remodelin'."

She took a step forward to peer into the bar, but Seamus hustled to block her. "No peekin'. It's going to be a surprise. I'm having a big party next weekend. You're invited, and you'll see it then in all her glory."

"So you're going to own a bar."

"Aye."

Charlotte chuckled. "*Aye?* Are you sure? You always sound more Irish when you've been drinking." Seamus had come from Ireland decades earlier. Normally, she could barely hear the lilt in his voice, but when he drank, he turned into a leprechaun.

"I'm sure." He winked and nodded his head towards the bar. "But Chuck may have left some whiskey behind. It'd be a sin to let it go to waste."

CHAPTER ELEVEN

Charlotte headed down the block towards Jimmy's, fishing her purse for her phone. Finding it, she called Declan.

"Hey, you," he said, answering.

"Did you know your uncle bought a bar downtown?"

Declan laughed. "He wishes."

"No, seriously. He's here now, cleaning things up. It's where that old dive bar was, Chuck's, down from Jimmy the Jeweler's."

"You're serious?"

"Yep. I just spent ten minutes talking to him about his hopes and dreams."

"He's been telling me he doesn't have the money to pitch in for food or rent, and now he bought a *bar*?"

"Maybe that's why he didn't have the money. He was saving up."

Declan grunted. "I'm going to kill him."

Charlotte paused outside Jimmy the Jeweler's door. "Hey. Are you at the pawn shop?"

"Yep. Blade and I are cleaning the things we picked up at Kristopher Rudolph's. Looks like the smoke damage wasn't bad at all."

"That's good. Are you going to be there a while?"

"Couple of hours. Why?"

"I'm going to swing over. I could bring you some dinner. Maybe something nice for you and Blade? I'm downtown. I could grab—"

Declan interrupted her. "Hold on. I know when I'm being set up. What are you up to?"

"Me? Nothing. I don't know what you're talking about."

I just need to talk you into hanging out with your crazy ex-girlfriend for a bit.

Declan sounded dubious. "Hm. Well, I'll be here. If you want to bring us something to eat, that's up to you. But food will in no way indenture me to you."

"Of course not. I'll surprise you."

He laughed. "That's what I'm afraid of."

Charlotte hung up and entered Jimmy's.

Like all the local businesses, Jimmy had his air conditioning at full blast. Nothing kept customers in a shop longer than hiding from the Florida heat.

She wrapped her arms around her body and rubbed her shoulders.

"Can I help you?" asked an elegant-looking older woman in a canary-yellow suit from her position behind the counter.

"Is Jimmy in?"

"Mr. Novak is in the back. I'll see if he's available."

The woman walked to the back of the shop, and Charlotte strolled along the glass cases. Most of the jewelry proved a little large and gaudy for her tastes, but she spotted an adorable pair of silver pineapple earrings she didn't hate the idea of owning.

She glanced up in time to spot a dark-haired man pop his head into the front of the shop. His eyes locked on her, and she waved, unsure how to respond. The man's expression relaxed, and he walked out to greet her, his hand extended.

"Hello, miss, I'm Jimmy the Jeweler. How can I help you

today? Engagement ring shopping, perhaps?"

Charlotte chuckled. "No. I wanted to ask you a few questions about Kristopher Rudolph."

Jimmy blanched. He took a step back as if the urge to run had struck him so hard he had to fight it.

"Who are you?" he asked.

"I'm Deputy Morgan." She searched in her bag for the badge Frank had given her and held it up for him to see.

I'll have to think of another way to carry this thing.

Pulling the badge from the clutter of her purse didn't have the *cool* she'd hoped to evoke.

Jimmy eyeballed her from head to toe. "Since when do deputies wear shorts?"

Charlotte didn't want to tell him Frank refused to give her a uniform. "Plain clothes division."

Jimmy nodded. Apparently, he believed plain-clothed deputies were a thing. Maybe she hadn't made it up after all. Maybe they *were* a thing. Or maybe she was the first. They could make a television program about her...*Charlotte Morgan: Plain Clothes Deputy.* She could almost hear the intro music...

"Did you find it?" asked Jimmy, his voice a whisper.

Charlotte snapped back to the issue at hand. "What?"

Jimmy glanced at the woman behind the counter and maneuvered so his back would be to her. The woman took a step back and pretended to straighten a display. She'd been leaning forward to better hear their conversation.

"Did you find it?" he asked again.

Charlotte's brow knit. "Find what?"

"The ring. The ruby and emerald ring."

Charlotte decided to pretend Frank hadn't already told her about the ring. "I'm not sure I understand what you're asking?"

Jimmy grimaced and touched Charlotte's triceps, the pressure of his fingertips coming just short of grabbing her arm. He eased her towards the front door, leaving her unsure if he wanted to speak outside, away from the prying ears of his sales associate, or if he'd decided to kick her out for invoking his costly and possibly misguided trust in Kris.

She was about to object to being manhandled when he mumbled, "We'll talk outside."

Charlotte pulled her arm from his touch and led the way through the front door and on to the sidewalk.

Jimmy squinted in the sun and pulled a handkerchief from his pocket to wipe his glasses. The quick shift from arctic air conditioning to Florida sunshine had caused condensation to build behind them.

"Kris has a ring of mine."

"You mean he had it when he died?" asked Charlotte.

Jimmy finished cleaning his lenses and put his glasses back on his face. He looked up and down the street to be sure no one could overhear them.

"Yes, he had the ring when he died. I need you to find it."

"Mr. Novak, it's been a week. Why didn't you mention something sooner?"

Jimmy huffed. "I told Frank about it today. I didn't hear he'd died until a few days after. And, to be honest, I wasn't sure what to do. If my insurance finds out I loaned him the ring, they won't pay out."

"So you want me to help you commit insurance fraud? Did you not see the badge?" Charlotte hadn't had the badge for fifteen minutes, and someone was already asking her to disrespect it. She pulled it from her purse and held it up again, giggly at the chance to do so.

Novak hissed his answer. "No, I don't want you to help me commit fraud. I just want you to find the damn ring."

"But what if we don't find it?"

"What do you mean? I'm telling you he has it."

"If we don't find it, you'll need to claim the insurance on it, right?"

Jimmy wiped his upper lip with his handkerchief. "Well, of course—" He stopped, his features wilting. "Oh. I get it. I just told you they can't know I lent out the ring."

"Right."

"That puts you in an awkward position."

Charlotte shook her head. "Not really. It puts *you* in an awkward position."

"Well, they won't know to ask you—" Jimmy thrust his hand in his pocket to find his handkerchief for the third time in a minute. The sweat poured from the top of his thinning hairline, splitting to run in rivulets across his left and right temples. Some of the moisture decided it didn't have time to pick a direction and instead dripped straight down, swan-diving onto the tip of his nose. He wiped it all away, and Charlotte watched it ooze back into existence.

"Can we just start over and pretend I didn't say any of this?"

Charlotte smiled. "Just tell me what you know about Kris. Is there any reason for you to think he'd done something with the ring?"

"No, I mean, not really... It's just—" He groaned. "I've handled this all wrong. I didn't realize he died until..." Jimmy trailed off. "Are you trying to tell me it's already too late?"

"No. I don't know. I know we weren't looking for a ring before. I know his wife has already sold the contents of his home—"

"*What*? Did she take the ring, thinking it was *his*?"

"I don't know."

Jimmy buried his face in his handkerchief and made another sweep of his skull with it. "Stupid. Stupid." He stared at Charlotte, and she imagined she could see the gears in his mind grinding.

"Is it possible he faked his death?" he asked.

Charlotte laughed and then caught herself. She sobered and cleared her throat. "No. That's definitely not possible."

"How do you know?"

"Because I saw his body, and believe me, he wasn't faking."

"What was it? Heart attack?"

"I'm not at liberty to say."

Jimmy wrung his hands together and peered up into the sky, squinting. "Why did I bring you out here to talk? We should have gone back into the office."

"When I asked you if you had any reason to believe Mr. Rudolph had done something with the ring, you didn't seem sure about your answer."

"I'm not. He seemed like a great guy, but—"

"But?"

"But I got an email."

"From who?"

"I don't know. It was anonymous. It said he was up to no good. I called him, but I couldn't get a hold of him. It worried me, but he already had the ring to show off at the parade, and there wasn't much I could do. I figured I'd get it back from him as soon as the parade was over. But I sort of lost track of time for a couple of days, and then I heard he was dead—"

"Do you still have it? The email?"

He nodded. "I can show you in the office. Thank god." He opened the door and strode through the showroom.

The woman behind the counter smiled at them as they passed, but Jimmy didn't acknowledge her. Charlotte smiled back before breaking into a trot to keep up with him.

"If the ring is so valuable, why did you give it to him in the first place?" Charlotte asked as they entered the office.

Jimmy sat down at his desk and hit his shift key several times to wake his laptop.

"You don't think I ask myself that every day?"

"I mean, you were donating it to the raffle, right?"

"Yes. I mean, no. Not exactly. He was going to pay me for it with money from the raffle right after Christmas. Wholesale cost, but I wouldn't be out any cash."

Charlotte scowled. "That isn't how donated raffle items usually work, is it?"

Jimmy shrugged. "I don't know. I don't think so. But that's what made this a win-win for everyone. That's what he said."

"So, you trusted him?"

Jimmy sighed. "I did. That's the worst part. He said the money was going to testicular cancer research, and I lost my father to testicular cancer..."

Jimmy turned back to his screen and clicked to his email.

"Here you go."

Charlotte leaned down to read. The note was short but warned doing business with Kristopher Rudolph would end badly. The author, 'Anonymous Christmas Elf,' promised to get back Jimmy's ring in exchange for a thousand dollars. If Jimmy waited to take advantage of the deal until after Christmas, the price jumped to two thousand.

Jimmy motioned to the screen. "See? This email sounds more suspect than anything Kris ever said, so I don't know who to believe."

Charlotte frowned. "Do you mind if I forward this to myself?"

Jimmy pushed his rolling chair away from the desk to make room for her. "No, go ahead."

"I might need to talk to you again." She sent the email to her personal account. It didn't feel right, but she didn't have an official deputy account.

Yet.

"And the ring?" asked Jimmy.

She straightened. "We'll keep an eye out for the ring."

The jeweler took a deep breath. "Thank you. I appreciate it. Hey, did Arnie get his car back?"

"What's that?"

"Arnie Burke. Did he get his car back from Kris?"

Charlotte recognized the name of a local car dealer. She'd grown up listening to him hawk his vehicles on local commercials.

"You're saying Arnie Burke gave Kris a car?"

He nodded. "Same deal as me. We offer our stuff to charity, and he pays us wholesale for it through the money raised by the raffle. Everyone's a winner."

"I haven't talked to Arnie."

Jimmy thrust his hands into his pockets. "I'd been meaning to ask him, but I was embarrassed for him to find out the predicament I put myself in."

Charlotte put out a hand to shake. "I'll look into it. Thank you for your cooperation."

"No problem. So I should just sit tight?"

"Give us a little time. I'll see if we can find your property."

Jimmy nodded and looked away. He muttered something Charlotte couldn't hear, but she could read his lips.

"Stupid."

CHAPTER TWELVE

The Previous Evening

The four gingerbread men sat in the truck as the driver slammed the vehicle into gear. He'd gotten pretty good at driving with puffy foam hands, but the way their heads wedged against the ceiling sometimes made things difficult.

"This is all your fault."

Gingerbread Two, sitting in the passenger seat, turned his head as far as he could before the cheek of his round face bumped into his headrest. "Are you talking to me?"

"Yes, I'm talking to you. You're the one who put the elf in his mouth," said Four.

"You said to shut him *up*. What was I supposed to do?"

"I dunno, maybe not *choke him to death*."

"How was I supposed to know he'd inhale the thing?"

"If I asked you to turn down the television, would you chuck it out the window?"

Two raised a mitt, straining against his seat belt to reach for Four. "I swear I'm gonna—"

"You two cut it out," said Gingerbread Three, sitting behind

Two in the backseat of the truck's double cab. "None of this bickering is going to help anything."

Four slapped at his own head. "Couldn't we have gotten better disguises for this? I can't breathe in this thing."

Two scoffed. "You'd rather have a stocking, I guess? Maybe a nice ski mask?"

"Yeah, now that you mention it, I *would* prefer a stocking to a freaking gingerbread man. I'd have mentioned it to you sooner, but I was afraid *you'd kill me.*"

Two turned his head so hard and fast his foam face ricocheted against his seat and nearly bounced him into the dash.

"I didn't mean to kill him!"

"Stop it!" screamed Three, again trying to keep the two of them from lunging for each other.

One made a hard left turn, and everyone had to stop fighting to keep their balance. "Look, I know the costumes are dumb, but they made sense at the time. It made it easy to sneak into the parade."

"A lot of good that did us," said Four. "We didn't get him there like we planned."

"No. And no, it didn't make a ton of sense to show up at his house wearing these, but they're all we got. We didn't think everything would take this long."

"We didn't think everything would *go* so *wrong*," said Four.

"It's not like we can get something else now," muttered One.

"Why not?" asked Two, sounding more curious than annoyed.

One huffed. "Do you not watch Dateline? How many times do you have to watch a guy on a closed-circuit television buying rope and shovels and plastic bags and gloves before you realize you *cannot go shopping for things like that.*"

"But all we need is a ski mask."

"In Florida? Could we buy anything *more* suspicious?"

"I don't think they even sell ski masks in Florida," said Three.

Four shrugged. "People down here go up north sometimes, don't they? They have to be able to dress for other weather."

"Who would leave Florida to go somewhere where you have to wear a ski mask?"

"I would," muttered Two. "I would leave Florida, where you have to wear these stupid costumes twenty-four hours a day. As long as I can get away from this place and never come back."

Three made a little yipping noise. "Ooh, what about pantyhose? Everyone buys pantyhose."

One shook his head. "It doesn't matter what we buy. If someone sees us and reports we were all wearing pantyhose on our heads, what's the first thing they're going to look for on all the local stores' cameras to prove it was us?"

Three grunted. "People buying pantyhose."

"Exactly."

"Yeah, come on, Karen, use your head. *Everyone* knows that," chimed in Four.

"I told you, don't use our names," snapped One.

"We're the only people in the car."

"Get used to it, or you'll slip."

Four snorted. "Fine. Whatever. It doesn't matter. We're all going to end up in jail, thanks to *Randy*."

"I didn't mean to kill him," muttered Two.

One pulled into Pineapple Port and crept through the neighborhood until they were a few houses away from Kristopher Rudolph's. He pulled over to the curb in front of a house with a "for sale" sign on its lawn. They'd parked in the same spot the night everything had gone so wrong. Feeling superstitious, One crept forward to another spot to take the curse off them.

Three reached for the door.

One held out a foam paw. "Hold it. We don't all have to go in.

You two stay in the back."

"What do we do if we see someone?"

"Just sit tight."

"Don't you think we look a little weird back here in these costumes?" asked Four.

"Just hold really still. They'll think you're a lawn decoration," said Two.

Three grunted her approval. "That's a good idea. But what if they don't see us? What if someone sees *you*? What if you get arrested?"

Gingerbread One adjusted his head. "No one's going to arrest me."

"Hurry up," said Four.

"Be careful," added Three.

One and Two let themselves out of the car and eased the doors shut. They scurried as fast as their thick foam legs would allow to the front of Kris's house and slipped into the screened porch.

Two peered out the way they had come. "I don't think anyone saw us."

"If they did, they're probably making a note to talk to their doctor about their medication."

Two chuckled. "They never mention giant gingerbread man hallucinations on the drug commercials."

"Try the door."

Two put a foam paw on either side of the doorknob and tried to turn it.

"I think it's locked."

"Is it locked, or can you just not grab it?"

"A little of both. But no, it's definitely locked."

One tottered in a circle until he faced the window facing the porch. He pushed up on the sash, only to have his covered hands slide across the glass. He took off one mitt and tried again. The window moved.

"This is open."

One pushed open the window and stood staring at it, mentally calculating his inflated size against the width of the window. Using his mitt, he rubbed the greasy handprint off the glass and then slipped back into the glove. He didn't move.

"What are you doing?" asked Two.

"I'm trying to decide whether it would be easier to try and step through or go in head first."

"I don't think our legs split far enough to step in."

"Probably not."

"Try head first."

One shoved his giant head through the window and fell forward, catching himself with his hands. He walked his hands forward, dragging his body through the window until he was clear.

He stood as Two grunted his way into the living room.

"We need light," said One.

"I have my phone."

The room remained dark.

"So turn it on."

"It's in my pocket." Two tried to remove his mitt, but he'd had Three snap them to his costume for him and found it impossible to release the snaps with no fingers.

"I can't get my mitts off. They're attached."

One sighed.

Two pulled off his gingerbread head and wrestled one arm out of the neck hole to then reach down into the body of the costume and find his phone. He popped out that arm with his prize, wearing the costume off-the-shoulder.

"That's the worst prom gown I've ever seen," muttered One, watching the empty gingerbread man's arm flop up and down as Two struggled with his phone.

Two flipped on his phone's flashlight and glided it from one side of the room to the other.

One gasped. "The place is trashed. We didn't do this."

"The television is gone," said Two, shining his light where the set had been.

One gasped again. *"The chest of drawers."*

They both tried to walk down the hallway at the same time, bouncing off one another and the walls. One huffed and took a step back, ushering his partner ahead. Two walked down the hall.

"It's gone. All the furniture is gone," he called back as One wandered around the kitchen. He'd wanted to check the drawers but had forgotten without Two, he had no light.

"Someone was here," said One as Two joined him.

"Who would tear the place apart and take all the furniture?"

"I don't—" One clapped his hands together. *"Noelle."*

"Noelle? The wife? You think she might have been here already?"

"What do you think? You think she'd let stuff she could turn into money sit in one place for more than two seconds?"

"I never met her. They were divorced by then."

"She made Kris look like a saint."

"So you think she took all our stuff?"

One shook his head. "I don't know. The way Kris talked about her—he knew what kind of person she was even back then. I don't think he would have trusted her to know where he kept stuff."

"No honor among thieves."

One grunted. "That whole honor among thieves never really made sense to me. Of *course* they'd all double cross each other."

"Right? That never made sense to me either."

The two of them fell silent.

"What are we going to tell the others?" asked Two.

One pounded a foam fist into the kitchen countertop. "We should have looked in the house *earlier.*"

"It's not our fault. The police were all over it. It wasn't safe."

One sighed. "Let's get back. If there was anything here, it's gone now."

Two nodded and raised his light to look for his head.

One and Two wrestled their way back through the window and scurried across the street to the car.

"Did you find it?" asked Four as they hopped inside.

"No. It's gone. Everything's gone," said Two.

Three's voice hopped up an octave higher than usual. "Everything? Did the police take it?"

One shrugged. "I doubt it. I'm thinking maybe Noelle."

"You think she could have gotten here that fast?"

"I knew we should have done this sooner," grumbled Four.

"We couldn't. The cops," said Two.

One started the car and drove them back, heading up the main shopping road that led to their hotel on the outskirts of town.

"What now?" asked Two.

"Maybe we can snoop around a bit and confirm Noelle took everything," said Three.

Four laughed. "How are we going to do that?"

Three turned to stare at him with her big blue circle eyes. "I don't know. Do you always have to be so negative?"

"Oh, I'm sorry. I tend to get a little grumpy when I might be arrested as an accessory to murder at any second—"

"Stop," barked Two.

The cookies in the back stopped arguing.

Two turned. "No, not you two. The car. Stop the *car*."

"Why?" asked One.

"Just do it."

One tapped the brake and, realizing he couldn't stop in the middle of the road, slowed and pulled to the right.

"What is it? We shouldn't be hanging out looking like this—
"

Two twisted to look behind them. "Back there. That pawn

shop."

One looked in his rearview mirror and saw the glowing sign. "The Hock o'Bell?"

"That's cute," said Three.

"I thought it was a taco restaurant. I'm starving," said Four.

Two pointed to a parking lot. "Pull in here."

One coasted the car into a large parking lot in front of an outdoor furniture store next door to the pawn shop.

"Go as far towards the pawn shop as you can," said Two.

One eased the car across the lot until the barrier between the two lots stopped him.

Two pointed. "Look in the window."

The lights were on in the pawn shop. All four cookies turned their attention to the store, and a collective gasp rose in the cabin.

"Is that the chest of drawers?" asked Three.

"It has to be, right?' It looks like it."

One nodded, though the others couldn't tell. "It is. I built the damn thing."

"What's the pawn shop doing with it?" asked Four.

"Maybe Noelle *was* here. She might have sold everything," suggested Three.

"Sounds like her," said One.

"We can go in and buy it tomorrow."

One sighed. "He has to have cameras. We can't go in there dressed like this."

"Just one of us can go."

"Which one of us?"

"I'll go," said Three. "My options for disguises are better. I'll mess with my makeup or something."

"I'll go. I dragged us all into this mess," said One.

Two shook his head hard enough that his costume moved. "I'm the one who killed him. I should go."

The other three fell silent. Three reached out and put a hand on Two's shoulder.

"I'll go."

Two began to sob, his cookie-brown shoulders bobbing. "I'm so sorry. I'm so, so sorry."

CHAPTER THIRTEEN

Charlotte looked at her watch as she left the jeweler's.

Time to swing by the car lot.

There was something else I was going to do. What was it?

She thought about it as she drove, but her brain kept ping-ponging back to the case. The list of people who might want Kris dead was getting longer by the second. There was his wife, who seemed opportunistic and not necessarily murderous, but who knew? Jimmy was technically a suspect. He could have gotten angry about the missing ring and lost his cool. Frank said the mayor might be in the mix—

What was I going to do? There was something...

There was the person who sent Jimmy the note warning him that Kris was up to no good. Who knew how angry *that* person was—if what they said was even true. Charging someone for help didn't inspire confidence in the helper.

Charlotte pulled into the car lot and took a moment to yank her concentration back from the suspect list. Her missing thought had *almost* returned to her when a young man approached and waved at her through the window. She stepped out of the car.

"How are you today, miss? How can I help you? Just let me

know what you're looking for, and I can point you in the right direction because here at Burke motors—"

Charlotte held up a hand. "I'm not here to buy a car."

The young man grinned. "That's what everyone says. But once you see our inventory—"

"No, I'm really not here to buy a car. I'm just here to talk to Mr. Burke."

"I'm Mr. Burke."

Charlotte scowled. The man in front of her was barely older than she was. The man in the commercials was quite a bit older. "You're Arnie?"

He nodded. "Arnie Jr."

She smiled. "Oh. I think it's your father I need to talk to."

Arnie Jr. hooked his mouth to the side and squinted his left icy blue eye. The redhead sported fair skin, ill-suited for a Florida boy. "He's not here. He's not here much these days. He got remarried a couple of months ago, and they've been doing a lot of traveling."

Arnie Jr. tried to flash a smile, but Charlotte found it unconvincing. Clearly, Arnie Jr. didn't love having a new stepmother. He wiped his brow with his hand, and Charlotte felt a motherly urge to drag him towards the shade.

She strolled towards the entrance of the showroom, where an overhang would block the sun, and Arnie Jr. followed.

"Do you know when he'll be back?"

He shook his head. "It's sort of an open-ended thing. Last I heard, they were in Marrakesh."

"Oh." *That took Arnie Sr. off the suspect list.*

Arnie exhaled with what appeared to be relief as they entered the shade. "Maybe I can help you?"

"I wanted to talk to your father about Kristopher Rudolph."

Arnie Jr.'s eyes popped wide. "What about him? He's running our charity thing."

"Your charity thing?"

"We're raffling off a car for charity." Arnie Jr. put a hand to the side of his mouth to imply his next sentence was confidential. "And we get a little publicity out of it."

"Of course. Which car are you raffling? Is it here?"

"It's not here right now. I can show you one like it..."

"Where's the actual car?"

"Kris took it. He's filming a commercial with it."

"How long ago was this?"

"About two weeks—" Arnie Jr. snapped his mouth shut and tilted his head. "Why?"

"Were you aware Mr. Rudolph died about a week ago?"

Arnie Jr. gasped. "Died? How?"

"Uh, there was a fire..." *And an elf...* Charlotte picked through her memory, trying to recall what had already been reported in the paper and what she only knew from being at the crime scene.

"Why didn't anyone tell *me*?"

"It was in the paper. Is there a reason you think you should have been told?"

"Because he has my car, that's why." Arnie Jr. dropped his arms to his sides like an albatross trying to fly with one sloppy flap. He remained rooted to the ground, the corners of his mouth sinking deeper by the second.

"I guess you didn't hear the news."

"I don't read the paper." Arnie leaned against a post, staring at the ground with his arms crossed against his chest, looking very much like a petulant boy. After a good pout, his head snapped up. "So, where's my car?"

"I don't know. If you give me a description, we can start looking for it."

"Are you a cop?"

"I'm a private investigator, but I've been deputized for this case." She pulled the badge from her bag and showed it to him. She attempted to retrieve it with more flair this time, but the purse still wasn't cutting it as a badge carrier.

"This *case*? Did someone set his house on fire?"

Charlotte grimaced, realizing her slip.

"No. I mean, the sheriff's office is just short-handed right now."

Arnie Jr. squinted at the badge. She feared the way she'd pulled it from her purse like a toy had made him dubious of her new far-reaching powers.

"I'm thinking about getting one of those leather badge holder things you wear around your neck," she added, slipping it back into her bag.

"Why don't you put it on a uniform?" Arnie Jr.'s tone had turned nasty. All his salesman's pleasantries had been tossed aside like a chewed piece of gum upon being told his car was in the wind.

"I don't have a uniform. I'm a plain-clothes deputy."

"Like homicide cops."

She grinned at the idea she'd already been upgraded to homicide. "Right."

Arnie glowered at her. "So Kris *was* killed."

"What? No, I didn't say—"

"Did the killers steal my car?"

"No, I mean—"

"You said you were a private eye, too?"

"Yes."

"Can I hire you to find the car?"

Charlotte took a breath, happy Arnie Jr. had left the notion of Kris's murder. "Well, like I said, I'm working with the police, so you'd be paying me for something I'm already being paid for."

Arnie Jr. ran his hand through his hair. "I hope it wasn't hurt in the fire. Were there any burned cars?"

"No, the fire was in his house."

"Oh, good. I mean, not *good*, but you know what I mean."

Charlotte nodded. Arnie Jr. repeatedly tapped his thigh with a balled fist, looking as if he was about to turn himself inside out with agitation.

"You seem pretty upset," said Charlotte, realizing how silly her sentence sounded directed at a man who may have lost a car.

Arnie Jr.'s eyes flashed with anger. "I gave the man a car. That car was my responsibility."

The emotion in his voice didn't sound like love for a car. She guessed he'd come just short of saying *Dad's going to kill me...*

Charlotte raised a palm to calm him. "I know, but you seem *really* upset."

Arnie smoldered for a moment before his shoulders relaxed. He leaned forward and dropped his voice. "I didn't clear the raffle with Dad."

"So you need the car back before he returns."

He laughed one loud, bitter-sounding bark. "Oh yeah. *Definitely.*"

"He would have found out eventually, wouldn't he?"

"Yes, but Kris told me they make so much money on these holiday raffles that he'd be able to pay me the wholesale cost for the car. No harm, no foul, free publicity."

Charlotte nodded. Jimmy had said the same thing. Kris's win-win offer to the retailers suddenly seemed much too good to be true.

"So your dad wouldn't have minded you selling the car wholesale."

"No. Plus, sales were already starting to pick up for the holidays, and it's a great cause."

"Sure. Cancer."

"Cancer?"

"The raffle. For testicular cancer research."

Arnie Jr. frowned. "The raffle's for wounded veterans and their families."

Hold the phone.

"Rudolph told you the money would be going to vets?"

"Yes. It's one of the main reasons I did it. My older brother was killed in Afghanistan. I thought Dad would be touched."

"All the money? Or just the portion of people playing for the car?"

Arnie Jr.'s brow knit. "I thought all the money. He never said there were different raffles for different prizes..." Arnie Jr. held up a finger. "Hold on. We have one of the posters on the wall."

Arnie Jr. strode to the front of the showroom and pointed to a poster mounted on the inside of the glass. The colorful sheet encouraged people to sign up for the raffle, where they could win a slew of gifts, many of them big ticket items. The car and the ring were featured, along with a one-week stay at a vacation property in the Bahamas, a pair of racing bikes, and cash. While it did tout all the profits would be going to charity, it didn't specifically mention *which charity.*

"Do you mind if I take that poster with me?"

"No, sure, I'll grab it."

Arnie Jr. jogged inside, and she watched him carefully peel the poster from the glass. He held the poster in front of him as he walked back to her, studying it.

"Now that you mention it, it doesn't say which charity," he said, handing it to her. "I never noticed that."

She took the poster. "Thanks. I'm going to go now, but I'll give you an update when I have one."

"Great. The photo of the car is on that poster, but if you need any other information—VIN number, whatever—I can get that to you. I'll text it to you. What's your phone number?"

Charlotte rattled off her phone number.

"Will do."

As Charlotte walked toward her car, her eye fell on a used Volvo 240 wagon. Something about the strange boxy shape of it appealed to her.

"How old is this?"

Arnie Jr. released his hold on the door to the showroom and

spun on his heel. "It's a nineteen ninety-one."

"Oh. Yikes."

"Ah, but you have a good eye." Arnie Jr. hustled over, eating the pavement with his long gangly legs. "It was kept in a little old lady's garage and was hardly ever driven. It only has fifty thousand miles on it."

"That sounds like a lot."

"For a car this old? They usually have at least twice that on them. And we went over everything with a fine-toothed comb. She's in great condition."

"You didn't say how much."

"Sixty-two."

"Thousand?"

"Hundred."

"Oh. Right." Charlotte felt herself blush. She'd never really gone car shopping before and was embarrassed by how little she knew.

"Can I open it?"

"Sure.

She opened the hatchback and peered inside. It didn't seem very worn, and the back wagon area would make a great place to throw Abby when they wanted to drive to a park or the beach for a walk. The exterior white paint had held up well under the Florida sun.

"Can I drive it?"

"Sure. I'll go get the key." Arnie Jr. thrust his hands in his pockets and stared at her, smirking.

"What?" she asked.

"I'm not here to buy."

Her brow knit, and he grinned.

"I told you that's what everyone says."

CHAPTER FOURTEEN

After a test drive and a promise to return, Charlotte hopped back in Mariska's car and dialed Frank.

"Frank here."

"We might have a con man on our hands."

"Who?"

"Rudolph."

"Dead Santa's a grifter?"

"I think so. I just talked to Jimmy the Jeweler. Rudolph talked him into donating a ring for a testicular cancer raffle, and then he took the ring, supposedly to display it during the parade."

"The ring Jimmy asked me about."

"Yep. Jimmy never saw it again."

Frank grunted. "Could be in the house somewhere. Or at the bank. The man was busy dying. He never got the chance to return it."

"Sure, but he also took a car from Arnie Jr. over at Burke motors, and Kris told *him* the charity was for wounded veterans.

"Arnie lost a son."

"I know. And Jimmy lost a brother to that particular form of cancer."

"I didn't know that. Hm."

"*And* Kris promised them both they'd be paid back

wholesale for the items, so they didn't mind ponying up big-ticket items."

"So you think he's telling people what they want to hear to get them to give him things he has no intention of giving back?"

"If this is a scam, I suspect he had no intention of returning the items *or* gifting them to raffle winners. He was probably going to run with all the prizes and raffle cash."

"Well, again, the man *died*. Who's to say the car isn't parked nearby?"

"There are a few other warning signs. Jimmy got an email from someone claiming Kris was a fraud."

"From who?"

"Anonymous. Literally. The return address was Anonymous Christmas Elf. He offered to get Jimmy the ring back for a thousand dollars."

"Anonymous Christmas Elf...and then Kris died with an elf in his mouth. Could the person who sent the email be the person who killed him?"

"It's possible. Maybe the plan was to kill Kris, take all the stuff, and then get the donators to buy it back?"

"Hm. But if you have the nerve to kill someone, you probably have the nerve to fence merchandise. The car and ring alone would be worth a lot more than a thousand dollars."

"True."

"Could we track the email account?"

"Probably not. It was a free account. Disposable."

"Well, this puts a whole new spin on the murder investigation."

Charlotte nodded. "Seems there are more people who might have wanted him dead."

Frank clucked his tongue like he commonly did when he was thinking. "I'll get Danny here to drive around and see if he can find Arnie's car parked anywhere."

"A car might be a little easier to find than a ring."

"Not for Daniel, but we'll see."

Charlotte chuckled and said her goodbyes as she slowed to make the turn into Declan's parking lot. She'd been on autopilot driving, but now something in the back of her head reminded her she still needed to sweet talk Declan into visiting Stephanie and poring through her fingerprint book.

As soon as she walked through the door of the Hock o'Bell, she remembered what she'd been trying to recall on her way from Jimmy's to Arnie's.

Dinner. She'd promised Declan and Blade food.

She stopped in her tracks. "Oh no."

Declan looked up from his desk. "I love it when people react that way to my place."

Charlotte smiled. "It isn't that."

"You forgot the food."

"Yup."

She spotted Blade behind Declan, pushing pizza into his mouth. She looked at Declan for an explanation.

"We ordered a backup dinner just in case."

Charlotte frowned. "Am I that predictable?"

Declan shrugged. "You get a little distracted when you're on a case, and I figured now you're a deputy, I should lower my chances of dinner delivery by another twenty percent."

"Great. I've been reduced to a mathematical equation." Charlotte's gaze fell on a giant chest of drawers. "That thing is even more impressive in better light."

"It's something, isn't it? Handmade by someone."

She walked to the bureau and leaned down to study each of the drawer knobs in turn. "Each one is a different thing."

"Yep. It's pretty amazing. It wasn't in the shop for more than an hour before someone bought it."

Charlotte straightened. "You're kidding."

"Nope. It paid for everything else in the house, so it's nothing but profit from here on out."

"You're a mogul."

He laughed. "Make up your mind. Am I a vulture or a mogul?"

"Today, let's go with a mogul."

Charlotte glanced at Blade. She wanted to talk to Declan about going to Stephanie's, but she didn't want to do it in front of his employee. The job might require a little light seduction, and she wasn't a fan of public displays of affection.

The shop's bell rang, and all eyes turned to the door. A woman wearing a ball cap pulled low entered the shop. She glanced up to find everyone staring at her, and the attention stopped her progress. Her gaze dropped to the floor.

"Welcome to the Hock o'Bell. Are you looking for anything in particular?" asked Declan.

"No." The voice seemed low for a woman with a petite frame. Pink nail polish flashed as she walked to the right, scratching her temple, obscuring Charlotte's view of her face as she passed.

Charlotte turned and looked at Declan with one eyebrow cocked. He shrugged and took a bite of pizza.

The woman walked directly to the ornate chest of drawers.

"How much?" she asked in her husky baritone.

"That's actually not for sale."

"Why not?" the woman's voice jumped higher, cracking like a pubescent teenager's. She cleared her throat, repeating the phrase in her original low tone. "Why not?"

"Sold. It's a pretty unique piece."

"To who?"

"Who did I sell it to?"

The ball cap nodded.

"Oh, I prefer to protect the privacy of my customers."

"Why?"

Declan's brow knit. "Why?"

Blade had put down his pizza, his curiosity piqued by the

woman's brazen question. Charlotte couldn't take her eyes off her. The questions didn't make sense, and, combined with the woman's odd voice and demeanor, she couldn't help but feel suspicious. She could tell by the expressions on Blade and Declan's faces that they, too, didn't know what to make of the woman.

The shopper seemed to melt beneath their gazes. "Nevermind," she muttered. Pulling her cap even lower, she scurried out of the store.

Charlotte turned to Declan. "That wasn't weird at all."

"Nah. Though I wish I could say that was the weirdest thing that happened to me this month. I had a guy bring in a stuffed ferret last week.

"Ew."

"Beloved family pet. He hated to have to sell it."

"You bought it?"

Declan pointed behind him with his eyes, and Charlotte shifted her gaze to Blade.

"*You* bought a stuffed ferret?"

Blade stuffed the last bit of crust into his mouth and nodded. "I have a little farmer outfit that fits it perfectly."

Charlotte looked at Declan. "Should I ask?"

"At your own peril."

Charlotte took a moment to find her composure. "So Blade, *why* did you dress the stuffed ferret in a little farmer outfit?"

Blade took a sip of his soda. "Because he'd look weird next to the girl farmer ferret without it."

Charlotte looked at Declan, and he shrugged. "I warned you. You're in the rabbit hole now."

Charlotte turned her attention back to Blade with equal parts eagerness and dread. "You already own a girl farmer ferret?"

"It's ferret *American Gothic,* 3D."

Charlotte pictured *American Gothic,* the famous painting of the stoic farmer and his wife posing out in front of their homestead.

She didn't have to picture it for long. Declan leaned down and produced a large wooden box tipped on its side, lid off. Two stuffed ferrets stood on their hind legs side-by-side, each dressed as farmers. Behind them, Blade had built a replica of the home from the *American Gothic* painting by Grant Wood.

"He's holding a little pitchfork," said Charlotte, pointing at the boy ferret.

Declan nodded. "Yep. It's a faithfully-rendered ferret-based *American Gothic* diorama. Now ask me why it's here behind the counter."

"Why?"

"Because we put it on sale here *yesterday,* and someone bought it. He's coming to pick it up tomorrow."

Charlotte burst into laughter. She'd been in the shop weeks earlier when Blade sold a mounted black-tailed deer head wearing a top hat he'd named Fred A*stag*, but the ferrets took his skills—both as an artist and salesperson—to a whole new level.

"Should I ask how long you had the first ferret before the second came to you?"

Blade shrugged. "A year, maybe."

"And was she dressed like a farmer lady the whole time, just waiting for her man?"

Blade scoffed. "No. What, do you think I'm *crazy*?"

Charlotte laughed. "Boy, I love Florida," she mumbled.

Blade tossed his trash into the can and wiped a speck of sauce from his mouth with a paper napkin. "Well, time for me to go. Nice to see you, Miss Charlotte."

"You too, Blade."

"Mind if I take a few of these with me?" he asked, stacking three pizza slices on a plate.

Declan motioned to the food. "No, go ahead. I don't want you to grow weak from hunger and pass out on a pile of badgers in tutus."

Smiling beneath his long mustache, Blade ambled out of the store with a final nod of an invisible cap.

Charlotte couldn't stop giggling. "The man has a real talent."

Declan nodded. "I just worry someday *I'll* end up in a diorama dressed up like Whistler's Mother."

Charlotte wrapped her arms around Declan's waist to give him a hug. "Hey, look, we're alone."

"If you count sitting in a lit glass storefront on a busy highway as *alone*. It's time to get out of here."

Charlotte gave him a squeeze and then grabbed a slice of pizza. She hadn't realized how hungry she was until the smell of baked cheese hit her.

Might as well relax a bit.

She could tell Declan was distracted and ready to close up shop. Maybe it wasn't time to bring up Stephanie *quite* yet.

"So, who *did* buy the chest?"

"I forget the name of the lady who bought it. I'd have to look it up. I remember she was from Tampa. Just happened to swing in while visiting a friend. She was so giddy when she saw it that I thought her head would explode. Apparently, she's got a real thing for Christmas, and a lot of those knobs look Christmassy."

"There are thirty-one drawers. It's like a giant advent calendar."

Declan nodded. "Except when you open a day, instead of chocolate, you get underwear."

Charlotte turned to stare at the bureau. "It is pretty. Someone took a lot of time with it."

"Kris, maybe?"

She nodded. "Maybe. Or his family. It has a family heirloom feel to it."

"I can tell you his ex-wife didn't care about it. She took my money and drove out of town like wolves were chasing her."

Declan folded the empty pizza box in half and started

cleaning up. The door jingled, and Charlotte turned.

Three human-sized gingerbread men stood just inside the door.

One of them held a gun.

CHAPTER FIFTEEN

"Uh, Declan?"

Charlotte remained still, unsure of the proper reaction to gun-toting cookies. The last person she'd seen in one of those costumes was dead, so she knew things were off to a bad start.

The gingerbread man with the weapon raised it.

"Get on the floor!"

Charlotte turned in time to see Declan straighten where he'd been bending over to pick an errant piece of pizza crust from the floor.

The gingerbread man waggled the gun. "Down!"

Now fully aware of the situation, Declan took a step forward to clear himself from the counter and moved to step in front of Charlotte.

"Freeze!" The armed cookie man took a step forward.

"There's no room back here to lie down," said Declan in a slow, deliberate voice.

"Well, get down *now*." The armed gingerbread man glanced at his friend, and though it was hard to tell, it looked as if the second cookie nodded.

Declan leaned closer to Charlotte and whispered.

"Do what they say. Don't be afraid."

Charlotte was surprised to find she had little control over her nerves. Even a detective's license and a deputy badge failed to make her cavalier about a gun pointed in her direction. She took a deep breath and wished she'd taken some sort of zen class to learn how to lower her heart rate at will.

"They still have to get down," said the second gingerbread.

The one with the gun shook it again.

"I said get *down*."

They lowered to their bellies. As Charlotte eased to the floor, she kept her eyes on the armed gingerbread. She could see a face inside the cookie's jellybean-shaped mouth, but the netting between the white icing lips obscured it too much to see detail.

He looked away from her to his friends. "Get it, quick."

While he held the gun on them, the other two gingerbread men ran stiff-legged to the ornate chest of drawers and began tugging it towards the door.

Declan made a quiet throat-clearing noise, and Charlotte turned her head to face him.

"It isn't real," he whispered.

"The gingerbread men?"

"The *gun*."

"Oh." She twisted her neck again to study the gun and noticed the odd, molded look of the weapon.

She turned back to Declan. "So why are we on the ground? Shouldn't we do something?"

"I don't want to risk you getting hurt."

Charlotte grimaced. She didn't like him assuming *she'd* be the one to get hurt. Granted, Declan had recently revealed to her that he'd worked for some sort of covert, quasi-government black-ops group before he returned to Charity to take over his uncle's pawn shop. She'd watched him karate-chop a thug before and had to admit he seemed more than capable of taking care of himself. Chances were good that he could kick the butts of marauding Christmas treats.

But then, who couldn't?

"I think even *I* can take out a cookie," she whispered.

Declan chuckled.

"Shut up!" screamed the gingerbread man with the gun.

He seemed excitable. Charlotte guessed the second cookie who'd nodded his approval earlier was actually the one in charge.

The other two cookies heaved and grunted in their attempts to move the giant chest of drawers. They could only drag it a few inches before they'd have to stop and move some other piece of furniture out of the way in order to make way for both the bureau and their poofy bodies.

"Without Blade, I would've been hard-pressed to get that in there. This is going to take a while."

Charlotte pointed to the gunman with her widened eyes. "Come on, tough guy," she told Declan.

Declan cocked his head to the right to gain a better view of the struggling cookies. "I dunno. I'm sort of enjoying watching them try to move it."

Charlotte grimaced.

Declan sighed. "Fine."

He jumped to his feet.

The gun-toting gingerbread man had been watching his friends. He turned as Declan rose to his feet and raised the gun.

"Stop!"

Declan grabbed the gun by the nose and whipped it out of the man's mitts. The cookie gasped.

"No!"

Declan tossed the weapon aside, and it skittered across the floor with a light, plastic-y rattle. He stomped in the gingerbread's direction as if trying to scare away a wild animal. The cookie yelped and stumbled back before slamming himself into the door and bolting outside.

Declan turned to face the other two cookies, who had both frozen as if hoping to blend in with the furniture around them.

"Split up!" screamed one.

One cookie ran toward Declan and the door, and the other shot to the back of the store. Charlotte leapt to her feet and blocked the cookie heading for the back from going any farther. Standing on the opposite side of a French provincial dining room table set from her, the thief feigned left, then right, as she mirrored it.

She glanced at Declan to find him holding the front door open for his cookie.

"What are you *doing*?" she screamed.

Declan's gingerbread waddled through the door. He glanced back to see if his friend was following and nearly stumbled before continuing across the parking lot in the same direction the first had run.

Charlotte's cookie doubled back and sprinted for the open door.

"Stop him!"

"Why?" asked Declan as the cookie ran past him. He stuck out his foot, and the cookie fell, rolling, before bouncing back up again and continuing to run.

Declan couldn't stop laughing.

Charlotte wove her way through the furniture to Declan. "Why did you let them go?"

He shrugged. "It got them away from you. And do you feel like spending the rest of the night here with the police over an attempted furniture napping?"

"No, but they wanted the chest of drawers." She heard her voice grow whiny.

"So?"

"So that's Kris's bureau. Kris's murder is still unsolved."

Declan scowled. "Wait, I thought Kris died of smoke inhalation."

"Why would they deputize me over a smoke inhalation?"

Declan jerked back his neck. "Why didn't you tell me?"

"Because I'm not supposed to share details of the crime with the public."

He frowned. "I'm not *the public*."

"You are, technically. In the law's eyes."

He arched an eyebrow. "Did you just seriously say *in the law's eyes*."

She giggled and felt her face flush with embarrassment. "Sorry. Frank told me not to tell. I didn't want to lose my badge. But to be honest, I was going to tell you tonight anyway because—" Charlotte stopped, realizing now was definitely not the time to tell Declan the favor she needed from him. "I just was."

"So Kristopher Rudolph was murdered? Definitely? Were there bullet holes or stab wounds or something?"

She bit her lip. "Not exactly."

"How then?"

"Someone stuffed an elf down his throat."

"What?"

"He suffocated on an elf."

"On an *elf*?" Declan's guffawed. "You're serious?"

"Yes."

He covered his mouth. "I'm sorry. I don't mean to laugh at the poor man's murder. This is just so weird." Declan ran a hand through his hair and stared across the parking lot. "And I'm sorry I let them go. But I doubt these guys had anything to do with Kris. They don't seem like pros."

Charlotte sighed. "Oh, they were involved, alright."

"How do you know?"

"Rudolph was wearing a gingerbread man suit when we found him."

"He...like the ones they were wearing?"

"Exactly like those."

"Oh."

Declan picked up the gun from the ground, holding it

gingerly in his fingertips. "We still have this. Maybe there are cookie prints on it." He started chuckling again.

Charlotte sighed. "Oh well. We'll just say you owe me."

He put the gun on a sofa table, slipped his arms around her, and pecked her on the forehead. "Okay. Fair enough. I owe you one."

"And I know exactly how you're going to pay me back," she whispered in his ear as he rocked her back and forth.

"Backrub?"

"Nope."

Declan released his hug and pushed back to hold her at arm's length. "Why do I have the feeling you knew what you were going to ask me when you showed up?"

"Hm?"

He pointed at her. "Ah. That's why you offered to bring me dinner. This has been a setup from the beginning. Did you pay those gingerbread men to come in here?"

She gasped, pretending to be offended. "*No.* Can't I just be a sweet girlfriend and bring you dinner?"

He pressed his lips into a knot. "You could, but you're not this time, are you?"

She looked away. "No."

"So what's the pre-planned mystery favor?"

Charlotte bit her lip. She glanced at the bureau and had an idea.

"I need you to *not* sell the bureau."

Declan's shoulders slumped. "I was afraid of that."

She walked to the chest of drawers and rapped on it with her knuckles, smiling at him. "Hey, let's find out what's so interesting about this chest of drawers."

CHAPTER SIXTEEN

Charlotte pulled a drawer from the ornate bureau. It slid out without resistance, and she squatted to peer into the hole left behind. There were no tracks; the drawer was just a wooden box that slid into a wooden hole.

"I guess you emptied all of these?" she asked, glancing into the drawer to be sure it was empty.

"Yep."

"Did you see the underneath?"

"Of the drawer?"

"Of the whole bureau."

Declan shook his head. "It was on its side for a bit, but I don't remember seeing the bottom, no. If I did, I wasn't really *looking*."

She stepped back. "Can you tip it?"

Declan stood behind the bureau and gave it a heave to tilt it towards him. Charlotte dropped to her knees to peer underneath. She saw nothing but the wooden underbelly.

"Nothing."

She stood, and he lowered it back down.

Charlotte pulled another drawer and peered in behind it.

Nothing.

She set the drawer on top of the bureau and paused before

adjusting the drawer, so the edge hung just over the front lip. She cocked her head.

The drawer was a good three inches shorter than the depth of the bureau.

"They're short," she said. She peered back into the slot where she'd removed the drawer. "I can see the back, but there has to be unaccounted-for space."

"False back, you think? Hold on." Declan jogged to the back of the shop and returned with an open-top canvas toolbox full of shiny metal tools.

He eyeballed the back of the bureau. "It looks like I can pull off this backing, but I want to do it carefully in the off chance I ever *do* get the chance to deliver this to the lady in Tampa."

The four corners of the plywood sheet covering the back were held tight by screws. Declan pulled a handheld drill with a Phillips head attachment from his bag and zipped them out, one after the next. Charlotte helped slide away the backing when he finished, leaning it against the store wall.

Like the front, the back of the chest had thirty-one drawers, but instead of knobs, each had a shaped indentation carved into its face. Charlotte's focus immediately dropped to number thirty-one, where she found the indented shape of a pineapple.

"It's the knobs," she said, circling back to the front of the piece. She unscrewed the flat pineapple knob and brought it to the back to press it into the corresponding pineapple indentation. It fitted like a puzzle piece. She pushed it in and turned it.

Nothing happened.

Declan put his hands on his hips. "I thought for sure we'd hear the sound of grinding gears when you did that."

"Oh, wait..." Charlotte realized that with the pineapple twisted and secured, unable to slip back out now that it had been turned, the shaft of the knob had become a knob of its own.

She pulled it towards her to reveal a short, shallow drawer.

A ring adorned with a large green stone encircled by smaller red gems sat inside.

She gasped. "It's Jimmy the Jeweler's ring. He gave it to Kris to use in the raffle."

"This is like finding treasure." Declan leaned around the chest of drawers to unscrew another knob.

One by one, they opened the hidden drawers, finding an item in each. Most were rings or other pieces of jewelry. One had a set of car keys. Charlotte pulled a pair of emerald earrings from the drawer that opened with the dove key.

"Looks like pretty high-end stuff."

"Why the elaborate chest? Was he afraid of being robbed?"

"Maybe. I think this chest was his retirement account."

"And if the ring he was supposed to give away at the raffle is already in a drawer, and all the other drawers still have prizes in them—"

"Then Jimmy's ring was never coming out of that drawer. Never being raffled to anyone."

"Think it's a coincidence our drawer's symbol was a pineapple?"

"Probably not. Though if he built this chest all in one sweep, then he was planning on scamming us thirty-one years ago, which seems unlikely."

"Maybe he made the knobs as he went."

"Or picked the cities based on the knobs."

"So the one with the pigeon could signify Pigeon Cove, Kentucky."

Charlotte's brow knit. "Is that a real place?"

Declan grinned. "No, I made it up, but you get the idea."

"Oh. Right. Could be. We could use that logic to maybe locate the owners of all these items."

"And whoever the cookies were, they knew about the hidden drawers."

She nodded. "Knew or suspected. Yep. Maybe they're working for Noelle. His wife could have known."

"But she's the one who sold me the chest of drawers. She wouldn't have done that if she knew it was filled with valuable jewelry."

Charlotte frowned. "Good point. Shoot. Maybe Kris has a family we don't know about? Or buddies who knew about the bureau?"

"Hm." He perked. "Hey, I think there's a Pigeon Forge, Tennessee. Isn't that where Dollywood is?"

Charlotte nodded. "I think so. Is your computer back there?"

"Next to the register."

"Let me try something."

She made her way to Declan's counter and typed "emerald earrings stolen pigeon" into the search on his laptop. The third result, after one on a Christie's auction featuring red 'pigeon's blood' earrings, was an article about a set of emerald earrings stolen by a Christmas con man who'd come to town.

She beamed, giddy to have already located a victim. "I think I found one. He's done this before in White *Pigeon,* Michigan. It's a tiny town. What drawer is the pigeon?"

"It was fifth from the end."

"So that would be the same year these emerald earrings went missing." She read a little further into the article and laughed. "Guess what the name of the con man was."

"Kris Rudolph?"

"Try Rudy Dancer."

Declan laughed. "Now, I don't know if I'm more excited to research the places he robbed or find out the names he used doing it."

"Give me another. Something recent." Charlotte bounced on her toes. Finding the key to unraveling the mystery of the chest of drawers felt a little like winning the lottery.

"Okay, second-to-last looks like a Christmas tree ornament. Inside is a sapphire necklace. Nothing too fancy, but it looks real enough."

"Penultimate," said Charlotte as she typed.

"What?"

"Penultimate. It means second to last."

Declan chuckled. "Whatever, *nerd*. Then I'll pick the third to last. There can't possibly be a word for that."

"Antepenultimate," she mumbled.

"Seriously?"

She tried a few different searches but couldn't find anything. "I'm not finding any towns called Ornament, and just searching for a stolen sapphire necklace, even paired with Christmas, doesn't narrow things down enough."

Declan squinted at the knob. "It looks like there's a little manger scene painted on the ornament. Does that count?"

"Hm. Nothing with a manger. Nativity? Wait, ah! Bethlehem, Ohio. They were hit as well. The guy's name there was Nick Frost."

"You're kidding me. I love it."

"And here's something. A lady being interviewed in this article talks about how sweet Kris—in this case, Nick—seemed. He found her dog when it went missing."

"And you found Aggie Mae's dog."

"Exactly. Tied to Kris's lamppost. There were scratch marks on the back of his bathroom door."

"You think he stole Aggie Mae's dog just so he could return it?"

"What better way to get a little free press and look like a small-town hero?"

"This guy was a piece of work."

Charlotte nodded. "I'm thinking whoever tried to cover up the murder by burning down the house knew about the dog and tied him outside so he wouldn't be trapped in the fire."

"So the fire was deliberately set by the same person who choked him with an elf?"

"Probably."

"But if the gingerbreads knew about the chest of drawers, why would they try and burn down the house with it still inside?"

"That's a good question. But I don't see how the gingerbread men could *not* be involved in Kris's murder."

Declan laughed. "Maybe they just really like Christmas furniture. They saw this in my window and lost their minds."

"That woman who came in had to be with them. She wanted the chest, and when she found out she couldn't buy it—"

"She tried to steal it." Declan pulled at his chin. "I don't feel like any of the gingerbread men were girls, though."

"I know what you mean. The third one never said anything but none of them moved like a girl." She laughed. "I feel sexist saying that, but we do move differently than you apes."

"Thank goodness. The world could use a little grace. Even in a gingerbread man suit."

"So that means we're dealing with as many as four people involved in this pawn shop heist."

"It's a gang of cookies. But when we catch them, I'm gonna tell them *Sorry, that's just the way the cookie crumbles.*"

Charlotte grinned. "And that makes anything that happens worth it."

"Absolutely."

Declan smirked. "But don't be too mean to them. After all, it could be their parents were thieves, and they're just chocolate chips off the old block."

"Ooh. Nice. But they have to stop *raisin* hell."

"Or their fortunes will change."

Charlotte nodded. "That one was a bit of a stretch. But I'm sure this case will be a piece of cake."

"Easy as pie."

Their straight faces dissolved, and they devolved into laughter.

Declan glanced down at the bureau. "Should we put all the

drawers back together?"

"No. I'll call Frank and get him to swing by and check it out. No sense closing it up until he takes an official inventory."

He nodded and began to gather his tools. "So, do you want to tell me what you really want?"

Charlotte felt her eyes widen.

How does he know I still want something?

She twirled a piece of her auburn hair around her finger and did her best to appear innocent. "Hm?"

"See? I knew it. My payback wasn't not being able to sell the bureau. What's the real favor?"

She walked towards him, snaking her hips from side to side and biting her bottom lip in a cartoonish rendition of a sex kitten. Upon reaching him, she placed a hand on his pec, and he closed his eyes.

"Oh no. Not the fake seduction thing. It's that bad?" he asked.

"What do you mean?" she murmured, kissing his neck.

"You want me to wrestle a lion for you, don't you."

She laughed. "No."

"Rob a bank?"

"No. Nom nom nom..." She pretended to eat his neck, giggling.

He laughed and wiped his throat. "Just spit it out before I actually start to fall for your feminine willies."

Charlotte grinned. "It's feminine *wiles*."

"Not when you're being that silly. Then you give me the feminine *willies*."

She laughed. "Fine." She took a deep breath. "I need you to take a photo of a fingerprint and compare it to some photos of other fingerprints in a book for me."

"Hm. That doesn't sound so bad. Little boring, but why me?"

"Because the book in question is, uh...under the care of someone who only wants to work with you."

"Who only wants..." Declan trailed off, and his eyes grew wide. "Oh no. Not *her*?"

Charlotte nodded.

Declan hung his head and sighed. "What if I wrestled the lion instead?"

Chapter Seventeen

"Where's your car?"

Mariska pointed the hose at her azaleas and glanced at Darla as her friend lumbered up the slanted driveway.

"Charlotte has it."

"Have you checked the possum trap?"

Mariska grimaced. "No. I want Bob to deal with that creature if we catch it, and he's off helping Hank with something."

"Helping him with his bourbon supply," said Darla, chuckling.

"No, something's wrong with Hank's golf cart, and Bob thinks he knows how to fix it."

"Isn't Bob the one who short-circuited your cart trying to add a spotlight to it for neighborhood watch?"

Mariska moved on to watering her enormous Christmas cactus. "Yep."

Darla walked down the side of Mariska's house and called back a moment later.

"I think I see something moving in there."

"Leave it for Bob."

"Oh, come on. Wouldn't it be nice to do it ourselves?"

Mariska's lip curled. "Not really."

"We can't just leave it in there overnight. Something might come and attack it."

"It would serve it right."

"Well, if you thought it was noisy before, just wait until a panther is rolling its cage around trying to figure out how to get to the chewy center."

"Oh, for the love of—" Mariska put down the hose and tottered down the side of the house to join Darla. As she turned the corner, movement caught her eye. Something furry was definitely in the cage.

"That was fast," said Mariska.

"It's the tuna we put in there. Probably stunk to high heaven after ten minutes in this heat."

The ladies crept towards the cage.

"At least it isn't that big," said Darla.

The creature's round ears flicked, and its head swiveled to face them, beady black eyes staring at them. The women froze. The mouth of the possum's needle-sharp snout hung open as if it were panting, revealing rows of pointy teeth.

The standoff continued for another ten seconds, and then the possum's eyes rolled back in its head, and it stiffened, flopping on its side.

Mariska put her hand to her mouth. "I think we killed it."

Darla blinked. "Think it had a heart attack?"

They moved in closer, eyes never leaving the animal. It remained on its side, unmoving, eyes closed.

Darla held up a hand. "Wait, I think I see it breathing."

"Maybe it just passed out from fright," suggested Mariska.

Darla patted her own ruffled coif. "It might have. I didn't have time to do my hair this morning."

Mariska gasped and slapped her friend's arm. "Oh, we're such idiots. It's playing *possum*."

Darla's expression expanded like a soaking sponge, and she put her hands on her hips. "Oh, *duh*. You'd think I'd know that growing up in Tennessee. I think the possum is our state bird."

"What do we do with it now? Can we ship it to Tennessee?"

"I don't think we need to go that far. We need to get the critter in a car. We'll take it ten miles away and let it out in the wild."

"How are we going to do that? I don't want to touch that cage with that thing in there. What if it wakes up and pounces?"

Mariska peered into the cage. One tooth hung out the side of the creature's mouth. The pink nose twitched, and she yelped, jumping back into Darla, who yelped herself in surprise even as she began patting Mariska on the shoulder, pretending her outburst was moral support.

"It moved," explained Mariska by way of apology.

Darla leaned in to inspect the animal. "That lady fell out of the ugly tree and hit every branch on the way down."

"It could be a boy."

Darla shook her head. "No. This one's a girl. Remember?"

"Is it the pink nose?"

"Maybe. Plus, she seems relatively reasonable."

"Well, thank goodness she's not a looker, or I might have fifteen babies living under there with her."

Darla shook her head. "No, I think you're safe with this one. She's a spinster for life, for sure."

Darla took a few steps back and stared down the side of the house to the driveway. "Let's put the cage in my car and drive it away."

"How are we going to pick up the cage?"

"With our hands."

Mariska crossed her arms against her chest and shook her head like an obstinate child. "Not a chance."

Darla looked up and to the left as if she were formulating a plan. "What if I tilt up the cage, and you slip a sheet under it, and then we'll drag it around the house to the car and scoop it up in the sheet to lift it in?"

Mariska wanted to find a problem with the plan, return to watering her plants, and forget about the giant furry rat in her backyard. She took a moment to find a way to poke holes through the idea and then huffed. "I hate to admit it, but that sounds like a good plan."

"Do you have an old sheet?"

Mariska nodded.

"Okay, you go get that, and I'll get my car."

Mariska glanced back at the possum. "I hope she doesn't wake up."

The two of them split. Mariska went inside and grabbed an old flat sheet from the laundry room. She enjoyed her air conditioning until she heard Darla pull up in her driveway, and then the two of them walked to the back of the house.

"Still dead?" asked Mariska as Darla made the turn first.

Darla nodded. "Still dead."

They stopped in front of the cage and watched the side of the critter rise and fall with her breathing.

Mariska gripped the balled sheet to her chest. "I don't know about this."

Darla patted her on the arm. "It'll be fine. I'll tilt up one side of the cage, and you slide the sheet under, and then I'll lift up the other side."

Mariska thought on it. "I'm not sure that works."

"It will work fine."

Mariska grunted. "Except for the part where I have to lean over for all of this nonsense."

"Get on your knees."

"Are you crazy? If I get on my knees, I'll be stuck there. And if that thing wakes up in the meantime, I'll be a sitting duck. She'll tear my face off."

Darla rolled her eyes. "Do you want to be the one who lifts the cage?"

"Absolutely not."

"Fine. I'll lift the cage and help you as we go. Ready?"

"Hold on." Mariska laid out the sheet flat next to the cage and then leaned over and grabbed the corner.

"I'll do this side," said Darla.

"But you're tilting the cage."

"I can do both."

"Okay."

Darla gingerly curled her fingers into the top of the cage and lifted it, tilting it to one side. Mariska wrestled the sheet as far under the cage as she could. With her other hand, Darla did the same.

The possum slid to the side of the cage but remained stiff as a board.

Darla set the cage back down. "That wasn't so bad."

"No, it didn't turn into a tornado of teeth and claws like I thought it would."

"See? This is easy. Now the other way."

They got in position, and Darla tilted the cage in the other direction. Mariska gave the sheet a tug. Nothing moved.

"That doesn't work. The cage is on it now. I knew there was something off with your math."

"Just pull it harder."

Mariska yanked on the sheet, and it jerked three feet past the end of the cage. The possum slid slowly to the opposite side of its prison, like a fat, furry, slow-motion Frisbee.

"I should get one of these for my kitchen," said Darla.

"A possum?"

"Yep. I could push it around all day with my foot and sweep up."

Mariska giggled. "Like a possum Roomba?"

"A *Possumba*."

The two of them collapsed into laughter. When they regained control, they took a step back to admire their work.

"Now what?" asked Mariska.

"I'll take this side, and you take that side, and we'll walk it around to the car."

Mariska wiped her brow. "I'm really starting to regret not hiring someone for this."

They each took a side and, using the sheet as a sort of hammock, hefted the cage. Mariska was surprised to find the creature was much lighter than she'd feared. She was pretty sure possums came in larger sizes. She'd lucked out with Scratchy.

They walked the caged animal from the back of the house to the side of Darla's car. There, they set it down.

"At least she's a petite little thing," said Mariska panting. "One more can of tuna in her, and I might not have made it."

Darla opened the trunk. "I don't think it's going to fit. I've got too much junk in here."

"So we did all of this for nothing?"

"No, we'll just put it in the back seat."

Mariska rolled her eyes. "This might be the dumbest idea you ever had."

Darla snorted. "Don't put your money on that."

Darla entered the opposite side of the car and crawled across the back seat. Mariska handed her one side of the sheet, and she took the other. Together, they lifted the cage and twisted and tugged it into the back seat.

Darla crawled back out of the car and clapped her hands together. "There, done! Now all you have to do is take it to the woods and let it go."

Mariska slapped her hand to her chest. "Me? You're coming."

"Actually, I have some things I need to do right now, but you tell me how it goes."

"Darla, please tell me you're kidding."

Darla laughed. "You should have seen your face."

"So you're coming with me?"

"Of course, I'm coming with you."

Mariska took a deep breath as Darla fished the keys from the pocket of her loose faux-denim shorts. "Do you want to drive or keep an eye on Scratchy?"

"I'll drive." As they switched sides, Mariska took the keys from her.

They slid into the car, and Mariska pulled out of the driveway. She sniffed.

"Something smells."

Darla nodded. "Our girl could do with a bath."

"She's a little ripe."

"The tuna can in the cage that's been sitting in the sun all day probably doesn't help."

They rolled their way out of the neighborhood, Mariska driving as if she were in a giant china tea cup, terrified any bump or rattle might spring her passenger to its feet.

"Still asleep?" asked Mariska as they pulled out on the main road passing through Charity.

Darla turned. "Yep. We're good."

"I'm thinking I'll go to that patch of wood up past the outlet mall."

"Sounds like a plan. See? This is easy."

They drove in peace for several miles, with Darla glancing into the back seat every few minutes to make sure their captive remained asleep.

As they waited at a light and Darla fiddled with the radio, something about the truck stopped on the opposite side of the cross street caught Mariska's attention. She squinted.

I can't be seeing this right.

Mariska blinked and rubbed her eyes.

It looked as if the car across from them was being driven by giant gingerbread men.

The light changed, and Mariska hit the gas, eager to get a better look. As the gingerbread man car passed them, Mariska's head turned to follow it. There appeared to be at least one other cookie in the backseat.

"Darla, did you see—"

"Mariska!"

At the same moment, Darla screamed, and Mariska felt the car lurch as her wheel caught in the soft ground off the right side of the road. She'd accidentally tugged the wheel right while turning her head left to track the gingerbread car.

"Oh no!"

The car lurched and slipped farther to the right. Mariska stomped on the gas, attempting to fight gravity and keep two wheels on the blacktop. A clatter rang out in the back seat as the cage flew upward and slammed into the ceiling.

Still accelerating, Mariska wrestled to keep half the car on the road as the other side bumped and jerked through the rough grass.

"What are you doing?" screeched Darla as the car rattled along the ditch. She braced herself against the ceiling with her palms.

"If I stop, we'll tumble sideways!"

They bumped over something hard, and, for a moment, it seemed time had slowed. The face of a startled possum floated past Mariska's vision, hanging suspended in the air between the two women. The creature's eyes were open now, blinking at her, wild with fear. The mouth had followed the eyes' lead and hung open, a slash of bright pink and pointy white teeth gnashing. The little claws worked the air, clutching nothing.

Mariska gasped.

It's out of the cage.

Mariska gave the wheel a mighty yank to the left, as much to right the car as to take herself as far away from the flying rodent as possible.

The possum bounced off her shoulder and flung in the opposite direction toward Darla. Its butt pointed at Darla's face like a bullet. Darla's hands flew up to block too late, and the creature smacked her in the face before landing in her lap.

Released from the rut, the car came to a stop.

Both women froze, staring at the possum on Darla's lap.

It grunted.

Darla and Mariska screamed.

Darla clawed at the door and rolled out of the car, dumping the possum with her. By the time Mariska had jumped from the vehicle, Darla was on her feet, still screaming and running around the back of the car. Mariska opened her arms to catch her friend as she collapsed into her.

"Its tail went in my *mouth!*" Darla couldn't stop screaming. Mariska shook her.

"You're okay! Are you okay? Calm down."

Darla caught her breath and pulled back to look down at her toes.

"I think so. I think I'm okay." She pushed out her tongue. "I swear I can still taste possum ass. That thing was *alive.*"

"I know."

"On my *lap.*"

"I know."

They peered over the hood of the car. Mariska spotted the possum's tush waddling towards the forest, where they'd planned to take it all along.

"It's gone."

The women braced themselves against the car, panting.

"I told you this was the dumbest idea you ever had," said Mariska.

"Now, I think you might be right." Darla turned and slapped Mariska on the arm. "What were you *doing?*"

"There were cookies."

"You can't be that hungry."

"No, there were cookies driving the truck that passed us. Didn't you see them?"

Darla huffed. "No, I didn't see *cookies driving trucks.* What are you talking about? Do you have some sort of mad possum disease?"

"There were gingerbread men. Driving the truck. I *swear*."

Darla cocked her head. "Gingerbreads like at the parade?"

Mariska gasped. "*Yes*. That's where I knew them from."

"It took you this long to place where you'd seen giant truck-driving gingerbread men?"

"Oh, shut up. I just nearly had my face clawed off by a giant rodent, thanks to you and your stupid ideas."

"At least you didn't get a tail up your nose." Darla frowned and forced her way into the driver's seat of her still-running car.

Mariska rolled her eyes and stormed to the other side. In a moment, they were back in the car and headed for home.

"Dumbest idea *ever*," muttered Mariska.

Darla snorted. "Worst driver, *ever*."

Chapter Eighteen

Declan stood in front of Stephanie's office door, wondering if he should knock or just walk inside. It was one thing, living in the same town as his crazy ex. He couldn't do much to stop her when she swung by his shop to taunt him. But it was a whole other thing to walk into her lair.

On purpose.

She knew he was coming. She'd had time to prepare.

Other people had crazy exes. It was practically cliché to have one. But not everyone's crazy ex used to be a black ops soldier. Not everyone's had a serial killer for a mother. Not everyone's flashed that strange little smile whenever chaos descended...

Declan's hand hung in the air, poised to knock when the door opened, and Stephanie stood before him, smiling, the arm of a pair of glasses inserted between her lips. She wore a spaghetti-strap camisole and a tight, short suit skirt. No pantyhose. Trademark high heels. Her blonde hair perched sloppily, pinned to her head with what looked like black chopsticks.

Declan mentally indexed the chopsticks as what they really were.

Potential weapons.

With her tousled look and professional-yet-revealing outfit, Stephanie resembled a naughty librarian, pulled from the pages of a nudie magazine like the one he'd found under his father's mattress as a kid—

Wait.

Did I show her that magazine?

As a child, Declan had shared all his secrets with Stephanie. She'd been his best friend. When he'd found his father's magazine...

I did. I did show it to her.

He remembered now Stephanie jealously ogling the size of the model's breasts, her own body still pre-pubescent.

Same color skirt. Same color camisole.

Declan sighed.

I shouldn't have told her I was on my way.

A mere half an hour's warning and she'd managed to transform herself into the physical manifestation of his young sexual awakening.

"You don't have to stand there like an idiot," she said. "You've been there three minutes."

He lowered his hand. "No, I haven't."

"I have cameras. I timed you."

Declan grimaced.

Have I been here that long?

He wiped his hands on his shorts. His palms felt sweaty. "I'm here for the fingerprint book."

"I know. Come in."

Declan glanced behind him at the sun, nervous he might never see it again.

The faint scent of alcohol teased his nostrils as he passed her.

Strange.

He scanned the reception area as she closed the door behind him. "No receptionist?"

"Briefly. Paul got himself fired."

"What happened? He walked in on you spinning a victim in your web?"

"He wasn't quite handsome enough to make up for how incompetent he was."

Declan nodded. "Unforgivable."

With a sweeping gesture of his hand, Declan paused and allowed her to lead him into her office.

Never show fear.

He followed her into the room.

If Stephanie was a dragon, and the building was her cave, her personal office was the treasure room. As he entered, Declan inventoried items of interest.

Antique gun mounted on the wall, probably working.

Three points of egress: Important! A window behind her desk and one on the side wall, in addition to the door through which he'd just walked.

A desk, full of drawers, containing unknown weapons.

A bookcase that could easily hide another cache of weapons.

What looks like a toy grenade, but knowing her—

She moved to a small table and rested her fingertips on a crystal decanter filled with tawny-colored liquid.

"Something to drink?"

"It's nine-thirty in the morning."

"You have a point?"

He noticed a finger of whiskey in the crystal glass sitting beside her laptop on her desk.

"Not like you to drink when you're in the middle of a campaign."

"What campaign is that?"

He hesitated, unsure if he wanted to reveal that he'd recognized her attempt to manipulate him with his own childhood memories.

"Making me come here in the hopes it would bother

Charlotte."

She laughed. "I'd hardly call messing with your girlfriend a *campaign*." She stepped closer to him. "Can't I just miss you?"

He held her gaze. "I wouldn't underestimate Charlotte if I were you."

Stephanie scoffed and looked away. "How is sweet Charlotte?"

"She's fine."

"Little boring, though, right?"

"Stephanie, I swear to—"

She laughed and held up a palm. "Sorry, sorry. Cheap shot."

Declan pulled a folded piece of paper from his pocket and opened it to reveal the oversized printout of a fingerprint. "Point me to the book I'm supposed to compare this to."

"Sure. Have a seat. I need to go over it with you."

He remained standing, and she shrugged. Taking a large photo album from the bookshelf, she placed it on the desk in front of him.

He glanced at her as she opened the book, and she flashed him a smile. An almost *shy* smile.

Something was off.

Declan's gaze flicked to the whiskey glass.

That's it. She's half drunk.

He didn't like it. It wasn't like Stephanie to take time planning her outfit and then muddle her brain and potentially miss a move on the imaginary chess board on which she lived her life.

Declan turned his attention to the book, but the gears in his head continued to grind out Stephanie's end game.

A disturbing thought occurred to him.

Am I reading too much into her outfit?

Maybe that's just the outfit she wore to work today. Maybe she didn't *care* if she was a little buzzed during her interaction.

Maybe she doesn't care.

That would be good. It didn't help him sleep at night knowing a wildcard like his ex might be somewhere out there with *him* on her Machiavellian mind.

But if that were the case, why had she insisted he come over? Why didn't she let Charlotte compare the fingerprints?

"Hello?"

He snapped his attention back to Stephanie.

He sniffed. "Sorry. Things at the shop on my mind."

Stephanie smoothed the pages of the opened book, standing close to him. When he peered down to look at the fingerprints, he couldn't help but catch a bird's eye view of her cleavage.

"They're fingerprints. I get it," he said, trying to move things along.

"Ah, but they're more than that. See this little code down here?" she asked, pointing at two numbers written in the corner of the first fingerprint. There were two fingerprints on each page, printed out and sealed behind the album's plastic pages. The second fingerprint on the page had three digits in the same lower right corner.

"Yes?"

"Code."

"For what?"

She curled her long fingers around the nearly empty glass and raised it for a sip, her eyes locked on his. "Not entirely sure."

He closed the book and picked it up to tuck it beneath his arm. "Great. Do you have a spot I can start on this?"

Stephanie put down the glass and grabbed him by the front of his shirt, the fabric balling in her fist. She tugged him towards her, staring up at him, her breath rising, covering him in a cloud of sweet whisky-scented air.

"You think I want you back, but you're wrong," she said, her voice barely above a whisper.

"Good. Glad to hear it." He tried to turn and go, but she tugged him back.

"I just want us to have *fun* again." She bit her lip and grinned as if the pressure of her teeth on her lower lip served as the only thing restraining her from kissing him.

He raised a hand and placed it on her upper arm.

"Stephanie, I'll be honest. Now that you mention it, there's something I've wanted to tell you for a very long time."

Her smile broadened.

"What's that?"

He leaned in and whispered into her ear. "You need to seek the help of a licensed, professional therapist."

She jerked back, releasing him.

"Take the book," she snapped.

"What?"

"*Take the book.* She can have it. She'll still do what I asked her. I don't need to hold the book over her. That's the kind of girl she is, right?"

She perched herself on the edge of the desk and crossed her legs.

Declan hesitated. Such sudden acquiescence had to be a trap. "I can take the whole book?"

She waved him away. "Go."

"Okay."

He'd nearly made it to the threshold of her office door when she cried out behind him.

"Wait!"

He turned, struck by the desperation in her voice.

She strode across the room to him, moving in heels with the ease another woman might have walking barefoot.

"What if I changed?" she asked, a crack in her voice.

"What?"

"What if I changed? What if I was good? Like Charlotte?"

Stephanie's eyes rimmed with tears.

Declan felt his cheek twitch. He'd seen Stephanie's crocodile tears too many times to fall for them again. But something about her expression...

Is this true emotion?

If it was, it was even more terrifying.

He sighed. "I don't know what you're up to, but I don't have the time for your games today."

He turned to leave.

She grabbed his arm. "I *need* you."

"Stephanie, we're not doing this again."

She shook her head almost violently. "You don't understand. It's different this time. I *need* you. You're the only one who knows me. Hell, *I* don't know me. You do. I need you to ground me."

Declan took a deep breath. "When I left you in South America, I asked you to come with me. I told you life there wasn't healthy for you. Not with your...family predilections."

"And I did. I came back."

"Months later. Months you spent down there, killing people under the guise of fighting the good fight. Months without me acting as your conscience."

Stephanie curled her hand into a fist and held it against her quivering lips. "But I did come back."

"You did. And I tried to mend the damage. And then you cheated on me and ran away with a polo player."

"But I'm back again *now*."

"That's not how love works."

"It has to!" She screamed the words, shaking both fists at him, tears flowing down her cheeks.

Declan wrapped his fingers around Stephanie's wrists and pulled her hands towards him, taking them in his own.

"Hey. *Breathe.*"

She closed her eyes. Her breathing slowed.

"Good. Now listen to me."

She opened her eyes.

Book still tucked beneath his arm, he held out her hands to

either side of him. Keeping distance between *them* and *himself* felt like the wise thing to do. "Steph, I've always felt responsible for you. I've watched over you since we were kids."

She nodded. "You've always been there for me."

"I know. But you have to understand. It took its toll on me. After you left the last time, I had to make a decision. Was I going to take care of you? Or me? I couldn't do both."

"Why not?"

"You're too much, Stephanie. You're not well. You make me not well." Declan heard the passion in his voice rise—heard the words before he said them—but he couldn't stop them.

"You're like a *disease*."

Stephanie jerked her hands from his, her mouth agape. She stood that way, panting until finally, her mouth snapped shut, and she spoke through gritted teeth.

"I hate you."

He closed his eyes and ran a hand through his hair. "I'm sorry. I could have worded that more kindly." He lowered his hand and opened his eyes. "But maybe not *better*."

She turned away. "So you give up? You're officially giving up on me?"

"I had to. I *have* to."

"Because of Charlotte?"

"Not because of Charlotte. I told you. I made this decision a long time ago. And doing it didn't mean it was easy for *me* to trust someone new. I didn't think I ever would."

Stephanie sniffed and wiped her nose on the back of her hand. "But you trust Charlotte with your heart." She turned back to face him, sneering. "Awww. That's *adorable*."

She spat the last word like a dagger.

He sighed. "I'm going to go. We're done here."

"Fine. *Go*."

Stephanie followed him to the door, on his heels like a shadow. He'd nearly reached his car when she called after him from the doorway.

"I can change. You'll see."

He paused. "I hope you mean that, but for *your* sake. Not mine."

She rolled her eyes.

"Whatever, Dr. Phil."

He slid into his seat. "Take care of yourself, Stephanie."

She remained in the doorway as he pulled out of his parking spot, one hand on her hip, the middle finger of the other prominently displayed for him to see.

CHAPTER NINETEEN

On Saturday morning, Charlotte had Bob drop her off at Arnie's car dealership to buy the Volvo that had caught her eye. She'd originally asked Mariska for a lift, but Bob overheard and insisted on taking her. At the dealership, he turned off his engine.

"What are you doing?" she asked.

"I'm going in with you."

"It's okay. I can do it."

"No, no. I'm a master at haggling with car salesmen. It's an art. They're animals, and you have to become an animal to beat them." He grit his teeth and flashed his canines.

Charlotte chuckled. "Okay..."

"What are they asking?"

"Six thousand. I did the research online, and it looks like a pretty good deal—"

Bob waved her away. "Nah, nah. Let me handle it."

They got out of the car, and Charlotte spotted Arnie Jr. heading toward them.

"She'll give you three thousand," Bob said as soon as he reached earshot.

Arnie Jr. took a sip of his coffee and cocked an eyebrow. "For *this* Volvo? Come on. It's worth twice that."

Bob grunted and crossed his arms against his chest. "Your dad would take it."

"No, he wouldn't."

"We bowl together."

"That doesn't mean you get to steal his car."

"Three thousand is a fair price."

"Can I ask what makes you say that?"

Bob shrugged, and Charlotte watched his bravado slip an inch. "It seemed like a nice round number," he muttered.

Charlotte laughed and put a hand on Bob's arm. "I was thinking five-five would be fair."

Arnie Jr. considered the offer. "I could do five-six fifty."

"Plus new tires," added Bob.

"It already has new tires on it."

"Plus floor mats."

"We don't sell Volvo floor mats."

"Plus a satellite radio subscription."

"They didn't have satellite radios when they built this car."

"I knew you when you were knee-high to a grasshopper, you know."

Arnie Jr. nodded. "Uh huh."

Bob elbowed Charlotte in the arm. "He used to have a problem with wetting the bed."

Arnie Jr.'s cheeks flushed. He glanced at Charlotte and then glowered at Bob. "Come on. That's not cool."

Bob shook his head. "It certainly isn't. Your poor mother, having to change the sheets every morning."

"Come *on.*"

Bob leaned forward. "Throw in free car washes for life."

Arnie Jr. sighed and turned his attention to Charlotte. "Fine. Anytime you want to bring it by for a car wash, feel free. Deal?"

Charlotte clapped her hands together. "Merry Christmas to me. *Deal.*"

Bob elbowed her again and winked, gnashing his teeth.

"Told you. *Animals*."

Charlotte shook Arnie's hand, and they started towards the showroom to fill out the paperwork. Twenty-seven years old, and she still had moments that made her feel like an adult for the first time. This was one of those times.

Arnie Jr. jerked open the front door of the showroom and walked inside.

Bob stopped, leaving Arnie Jr. holding the door, air conditioning blasting out of the showroom to cool them. He turned and stared back at the Volvo.

"Your mother had a car just like that, you know."

Charlotte turned and grinned at her new car that gleamed beneath Florida's morning sun. She'd been drawn to the vehicle and hadn't known why. Now that Bob had made the connection for her, the threads of her memories wove together, completing the picture.

"She did?" she whispered, but she already knew it to be true. She'd been so young, but she could picture the car now. Before her mother died. Before she went to live with her grandmother in Pineapple Port. Before her grandmother died, leaving her an orphan to be raised by Mariska and Bob, Darla and Frank, and the rest of the community. Before any of that, she could remember getting into a white Volvo, her mother buckling her in. She remembered her mother holding out a cup with a straw. She could taste it.

Chocolate milkshake.

She turned to find Bob holding the door open for her. Arnie Jr. had given up on chivalry and stormed inside.

"I remember Mom taking me to get hamburgers for dinner in a car like that."

He nodded. "Your grandmother had her Lincoln. Didn't need a second car. She sold the Volvo shortly after you came to live with her."

Charlotte glanced back at the car. "Huh. Isn't that funny?"

After buying the car, Charlotte drove it directly to the home of Assistant District Attorney Jason Walsh, ready to start the first day of her assignment for Stephanie. The previous night she'd set up motion cameras outside his front and back doors and knew he hadn't done much other than pick up his newspaper in striped pajama pants.

From her parking spot across the street and down the block, she could see him through his front window, reading his paper and drinking coffee. His wife walked back and forth in a t-shirt and tights. It appeared as if she were interacting with something too low for Charlotte to see. A kid or a dog. She wasn't sure which. Stephanie hadn't provided her with any background information.

Just watch him. And let me know if he gets anywhere near this woman. If he does, I need to know every word they say. That's all Stephanie had said before sending her an email with a name, photo, and address in Ybor City. Now Charlotte prayed Jason wouldn't get anywhere near the woman in Ybor City. She had no idea how she was going to listen to their conversation if he did.

Charlotte checked her watch. It was nearly ten a.m. At that very moment, Declan was probably sitting in the demon seed's office, comparing the fingerprint she'd given him to Stephanie's book.

She felt bad.

Her phone rang, and she saw it was Declan calling.

"That was fast," she said, answering.

"I didn't have to stay. She gave me the book."

"The whole book?"

"Yep."

"Wow. Aren't you smooth. Good job. You didn't have to sell your soul or anything, did you?"

He chuckled. "I got that back from her years ago."

His voice lacked energy.

"You sound tired."

Declan cleared his throat. "Sorry. She was sort of a mess. It can be exhausting dealing with her highs and lows."

Charlotte frowned. "I'm sorry I put you through that. I was desperate."

"It's fine. I'm used to it. Out of practice but used to it. And this time, I could see the light at the end of the tunnel."

"What's that?"

"You."

She smiled broadly enough to imagine he could see it through the phone. "You're okay?"

"Of course. I'm fine."

"And her?"

He sighed. "I don't know."

"You don't know? It was that bad?"

"No. I mean, she'll be fine. She's always fine. She was a little drunk."

"At ten a.m.?"

"More like nine. Where are you?" Charlotte could tell he wanted to change the subject.

"I'm sitting outside Assistant D.A. Jason Walsh's house, as promised. I have to watch him night and day until Monday."

"It's only Saturday. You can't *not* sleep for two days."

"I assume *he'll* sleep. Then I'll catnap."

"But you won't know if he leaves the house."

"I set up motion cameras next to his front and back doors. It will ring on my phone and wake me up if he tries to leave."

Declan whistled. "Look at you. You're like a real private eye now."

"And deputy."

"Right. I almost forgot. So I guess I won't see you for a couple of days. Maybe I could swing by and hang out with you."

"You'll have to look for a white Volvo 240 wagon."

"What do you mean?"

"I bought a car."

"You bought a *car*?"

"It's my Christmas present to myself."

"What kind?"

"A Volvo. It's old, but it's in really good shape."

"Congratulations. I guess Mariska will be happy to not have to wonder if her car is in her driveway or not."

Charlotte chuckled. "What do you have planned for your day?"

"Frank's coming by to gather everything from the chest of drawers and dust for fingerprints or whatever needs to be done."

"Keep an eye out for rogue gingerbreads."

"Definitely. If I have some time, I'll see if I can find a match for your fingerprint, too."

Charlotte suffered another pang of guilt. "Oh, you don't have to. We can give the book to Frank, and he can get Daniel to do it. The book is my Christmas gift to him."

She heard Declan's shop bell ring in the background.

"Speaking of Christmas gifts, what did you get me?" he asked.

The smile slid from her face. *I have no idea.*

"I'll never tell," she said instead. "What did you get me?"

"Well, I *had* gotten you a Volvo, but I guess I'll have to take that back now."

She laughed.

"I've got to go. Frank's here to look at the bureau—oh, hold on, he wants to talk to you."

"I've got some updates for you," said Frank in his gruff voice a moment later.

"Great. What's new?"

"Harlan confirmed your con theory."

"The mayor knew about him?"

"Says after Kris died, he started to piece together things in his head and realized he might have been recommending the man to businesses in town without really knowing who he was."

"So that's why he's been acting weird."

"Yep. Doubt he killed him, though. He's just scared to death the town will find out he let the wolf in the house, and he'll lose his next election. And we found out who sent that email to Jimmy."

"Who?"

"Kris. The techs found it on the laptop we took from his office."

Charlotte scowled. "Wait—You're saying Kris sent an email to Jimmy warning him not to trust *him*? That doesn't make sense."

"It does if he was double-conning them."

Charlotte gaped. "He was going to con them and then con them *again* into paying him *more* to keep from being conned?"

"By the time they realized what was going on, he'd be gone."

Charlotte shook her head. "What a *jerk*."

"That's one word for it. On the upside, Daniel found Arnie Jr.'s missing car. It was parked in a shopping center parking lot one town over."

"Oh, that's good."

"Yep. Here's your man."

Declan's voice returned. "Okay, gotta go."

Charlotte sighed. "Shoot. Feel free to call back anytime you're bored. I have a lot of time to kill here."

"Okay. Will do. Hey..."

"Yeah?"

"Love you."

Charlotte made a little squeaking noise in the back of her throat as her jaw worked but no words formed.

"Later. Bye." Declan disconnected.

"I love you, too—"

He was gone.

Charlotte lowered her phone to her lap.

Wow.

What did Stephanie do or say to him that he trotted out the L-word?

Declan's tone hadn't sounded like guilt or like he was trying to convince himself his words were true. If she had to pick a word to describe his tone, it would be *sincere*.

Unable to wipe the smile from her face, Charlotte settled into her surveillance. Jason remained in clear sight, shoveling eggs into his mouth. It didn't look as if he had plans to ruin Stephanie's case today, but she'd have to watch him either way.

I need to think of a Christmas gift for Declan.

Sitting quietly in utter forced boredom would be good for thinking.

She ran her hand over the leather of the passenger seat and sighed. The last thing she needed to be doing now was following around an assistant district attorney. Things were heating up in the Kris Rudolph case. She wanted to be searching for the gingerbreads and interviewing people, if for no other reason than to flash them her deputy badge.

Charlotte heard her back door open and whirled to find Darla and Mariska sliding into her backseat.

"What are you two doing here?"

"We brought you breakfast," said Darla, handing her a Tupperware.

Charlotte stared at the clouded image of pierogies and kielbasa pressed against the lid of the container. Mariska could sneeze, and a pan of pierogies and kielbasa would appear.

Mariska closed her door, and Charlotte winced at the noise. "How did you find me?"

"Bob told me about the car and that you were on a stakeout, and here we are."

"I don't remember telling Bob who I was watching."

Mariska scowled. "Of course you did."

"How else could we have found you?" asked Darla,

slamming shut her own door.

Charlotte winced again. She was embarrassed she hadn't heard the ladies coming. They had to have slammed their own doors, too. She'd been distracted. It must have been the same time Declan said *I love you...*

She glanced down the road to see if all the slamming had caught Jason's attention. He remained intent on his paper. She slid a little lower in her seat. "It's hard to be inconspicuous when you have ladies delivering pierogies to your stakeout car and slamming doors left and right."

"Sorry. Did Bob tell you your mother had a car like this?" asked Mariska.

She nodded. "He did."

"It's in lovely shape. Bob said you were a very good negotiator, too."

Charlotte tittered. "Bob did all the hard work. He got me free car washes for life."

Mariska nodded. "He's very good with car salesmen."

Darla skootched to the end of her seat and peered through the front window. "How's it going? Did your victim make any suspicious movements yet?"

"He's not my *victim*. He's my *target*. Or *subject*. And no. He hasn't done anything but drink coffee, eat eggs, and read his paper."

Darla clapped her hands together. "This is so exciting. It makes me feel like a spy."

Mariska poked Darla in the shoulder. "You need to tell Frank we need badges."

Charlotte glanced in her rearview. "Would you two like to be my secret operatives today?"

"What do you mean?"

Charlotte twisted to face them. "First, let's get one thing straight. I never told Bob who I was surveilling today. You drove around until you saw this car, didn't you?"

Mariska's face morphed into the passive, expressionless mask she adopted whenever she wasn't being *exactly* truthful.

"Bob told us where you were."

"Because *he* followed me."

Mariska pressed her lips together and looked away.

Darla slapped the seat next to her. "It's so nice being in a car without a possum in it."

Charlotte turned. "A possum? What are you talking about?"

"We trapped a possum and drove it to the forest down from the outlet mall to release it. We were almost there when Mariska thought she saw giant cookies driving a truck and almost killed us both."

Mariska scowled. "I *did* see giant cookies. And it was a stupid idea."

Charlotte's eyes grew wide. "Giant cookies? Gingerbread men?"

Mariska gasped. "Yes! How did you know?"

"Three gingerbread men tried to rob Declan's shop yesterday." She left out the part about Kris Rudolph being found dead in a gingerbread costume.

"I told you," Mariska slapped Darla's arm. "I told you I saw giant gingerbread men in that truck."

Darla leaned forward and put her hand on Charlotte's shoulder. "You know you shouldn't encourage her craziness. She needs our help."

Mariska slapped her friend a second time. "I'm not *crazy*."

Charlotte decided she should sidetrack them before they started wrestling in the back of her new Volvo. "What kind of vehicle were they in?"

Mariska pinched her lips into a knot. "It was a truck, but I don't know what kind. I was so distracted by the cookies...I want to say black? Yes, I'm sure of the color because I remember thinking it wasn't very Christmassy for gingerbreads. But I don't know what *kind* of truck. Something newish. It looked like the sort that has a back seat. *Big*."

Charlotte nodded, processing this new information. Now she had two vehicles to find. She grabbed her phone. "I'm going to forward Darla the text Arnie Jr. sent me with the details of his missing car—" Mariska opened her mouth to speak, and Charlotte cut her short. "I'm sending it to Darla because your phone only accepts faxes from nineteen seventy-two."

Mariska humphed.

"While you drive around, keep an eye out for the gingerbreads' truck, too. Might as well kill two birds if we can."

Darla's phone dinged, and she glanced at it. "Got it. It will have to wait about twenty minutes, and then we'll be on the case."

"Why do we have to wait?" asked Mariska.

"We have to go find Frank and make him give us deputy badges in case we have to make a citizen's arrest."

CHAPTER TWENTY

Gingerbread One used his key to enter the motel room and rubbed his gray head with the other hand.

He'd driven by the pawn shop and knew they were done. Nothing had turned out like he had planned. He felt beaten and old. It was time to go home.

Old Kris had won again.

"How'd it go?" asked Four. With his fiery red hair and boundless energy, he looked a lot more confident out of his costume. In his costume, the top of his foam head drooped due to his diminutive stature, making his cookie look as if it was depressed and staring at the ground.

One tossed the car keys on the bureau and pulled a chair away from the table in front of the window to sit. "There was a police car parked out front. They had opened the back of the bureau. If there was anything in there, they found it."

"Maybe they won't know how to open the drawers," suggested Four.

One snorted a laugh. "Once you find the boxes in the back, a child could figure out how to open them."

"You said there was a trick to it."

He nodded. "There is. But I didn't say it was a difficult trick."

He looked up and spotted Two standing outside the bathroom door, listening to their conversation.

"So we're done?" Two asked. His voice remained monotone. One couldn't tell if he looked forward to leaving or considered it their final failure.

One picked at the cracked top of the laminated table. "We're done. There's nothing left to do. Maybe they'll manage to get whatever they find in the bureau back to the owners."

"We can send an anonymous note giving them hints about the places we know," suggested Four.

One frowned. "I don't know if that's a good idea. We don't want anyone to know we were involved. They might put two and two together. There's still a murder to answer for."

Four swung at the air. "This was over the moment that bastard choked. Without him to tell us where he put the money, the cars—"

Two's shoulders slumped.

Four threw his back against the wall and stared up at the ceiling. "Maybe they'll find money in the chest of drawers. Maybe a lot of it."

A piece of the table gave way beneath his fiddling, and One pushed it back into place, embarrassed he'd been vandalizing the room. "Maybe."

Two headed for the door. "I'm going to go look for Karen. I think she went to get coffee."

Two walked by and left the room.

One looked at Four. "How's he doing?"

Four shrugged. "Not good. I caught him crying this morning."

One sighed and leaned over to rest his forearms on his knees. "What a mess. I just wanted to get our things back. Give that bastard what he deserved."

"You could say he got that."

"I meant prison."

"I know. Still."

"We'll head for home when they get back." One's gaze settled on the top of the bureau. He scowled.

"Where are the keys?"

"Huh?"

"I threw the truck keys there. Next to the lamp."

Four looked at the empty bureau top. "I don't know—" He glanced at the door. *"Randy."*

One stood and flung open the front door. He spotted the back of his black double-cab pickup truck pulling out of the parking lot and onto the street.

"He's got the truck."

"What is he up to now?"

One sighed. "I have an idea."

CHAPTER TWENTY-ONE

Jason Walsh finished his coffee and disappeared somewhere in the bowels of his home. The motion detection camera Charlotte set in the crook of a tree overlooking Walsh's fenced backyard triggered, and Charlotte watched the live video feed on her phone. Jason exited the back of his house in a faded red t-shirt and cargo shorts. He walked out of frame. Ten minutes later, he appeared in his front yard pushing a lawn mower.

Charlotte thunked her head against the Volvo's headrest and closed her eyes. As long as she could hear the lawnmower, she knew where Jason was.

"Master criminal," she mumbled to herself.

Stephanie had her watching Jason, the all-American dad, on the weekend.

She sat up.

Was that the point? Had Stephanie wanted to mess with her? Force her to do something boring? Keep her away from Declan so she could work her claws into him somehow?

She sighed.

It didn't matter. Declan was a grown man who could take care of himself, even against the likes of Stephanie. And if Stephanie's point was to bore Charlotte to tears in exchange for the fingerprint book, then that was the price she had to pay. At least they had the whole book now. She wouldn't have to make another compact with the devil to get the second half.

She could use the time in her new car to think. For one, she hadn't come up with a Christmas present for Declan yet, and she was running out of time.

Plus, she had the gingerbread men to consider. It couldn't be a coincidence they'd found Kristopher Rudolph in a gingerbread suit, and then identical cookies tried to rob Kris's unique chest of drawers from Declan's shop. Then Mariska spots gingerbreads driving through town? They *had* to be the ones responsible for Kris's death.

There had been three cookies at Declan's. Though, she felt confident the woman who came into the Hock o'Bell right before the robbery attempt was connected. She'd been too squirrelly. Too desperate to hide her face from them.

A truck. Mariska had seen a truck. And the gingerbreads had tried to take the whole bureau. They couldn't fit that chest of drawers in a sedan; they had to have a truck. They hadn't parked in the Hock o'Bell lot, but they couldn't have parked very far away if their plan was to carry off that monster of a bureau. Maybe if Frank collected the CCTV footage from the shops around Declan's, he could find the gingerbreads' truck and get a license plate—

Hold on.

CCTV.

Tilly. How did I forget Tilly?

While Pineapple Port had no official security other than the volunteer neighborhood watch—which served more as an excuse to drive around on golf carts drinking cocktails than any real security measure— Tilly's personal network of cameras and logs *more* than covered the area. She had the neighborhood wired with cameras and kept a meticulous log of comings and goings, known and feared as The Book.

No one had an affair, a tete-a-tete, or a bad hair day without Tilly knowing.

Granted, Tilly's inspiration for the network was her family's past ties to organized crime and her fear of being found, but it still proved a good resource for Charlotte.

Maybe Tilly had caught an image of a truck in the neighborhood on the night of Kris's murder. If Tilly hadn't captured the vehicle or the cookies digitally, maybe she'd jotted down *something* that would help.

Jason started down another strip of the lawn as Charlotte called Tilly.

"Hello?" Tilly answered in her unique raspy baritone cultivated through years of smoking.

"Tilly, it's Charlotte. I need you to check your tapes for a truck entering or leaving Pineapple Port last Saturday night.

"The night of the fire?"

"Exactly. Do you have footage of Kris's house?"

"No. I scaled back the cameras. I don't have as much time to worry about them now. Harry is always taking me on trips."

Charlotte sighed. Tilly had recently reunited with an old love, and it seemed the romance had bloomed. Unfortunately, her new relationship had eaten into her surveillance time.

"I think I'm looking for a black truck sometime before or after the time of the fire."

"Oh, you know what? I might have that. Hold on."

Charlotte heard rustling on the other end of the line.

"I remembered it because it was Nebraska. Don't see a lot of those."

"What was Nebraska?"

"The license plate of the truck. I wanted to add it to my license plate game sheet. I've got it mostly filled out except for Hawaii and some of the Midwest. All these long drives Harry takes me on. Game changer. I spotted an Iowa the other day."

Charlotte allowed Tilly to rattle off the states she was

missing on her sheet while her mind wandered back to the truck.

Nebraska. The cookies had come thousands of miles to kill Kris and steal a bureau?

"What color was the truck?"

Tilly droned on in her gravelly baritone. "...Montana's always a hard one, what?"

"What color was the Nebraska truck?"

"Eh. Hold on. I'm almost there... Black by the look of things. Hard to tell exactly at night, but I'm pretty sure it's black. That's what I wrote down in The Book."

"Thank you, can you give me that plate?"

"Sure."

Tilly rattled off the plate number, and Charlotte chanted it in her head so she wouldn't forget.

"Okay. Got it. Thank you, Tilly."

"No problem, kid."

Charlotte hung up and typed the number into her phone's notes so she wouldn't forget it. She'd give it to Frank to—

She realized the sound of the lawn mower had stopped and looked up to find Jason gone.

A second later, the back camera tripped, and she watched him reenter the house. He'd been out of frame. Probably putting away the lawn mower.

Charlotte tapped the faux leather backing of her cell phone cover against her teeth, deep in thought. *Nebraska.* Someone, possibly four giant cookies, drove from Nebraska to Florida to kill Kristopher Rudolph.

Why?

The previous evening she and Declan had spent some time researching reports of Christmas scams with missing items that matched treasure in the drawers. They'd found a handful, all of them in small towns. Sometimes *tiny* towns.

Charlotte used her phone to search for reported Christmas scams in Nebraska. Nothing came up. Of course, if Kris ran a con every year and he was on year thirty-one, the Nebraska scam could have happened during the very earliest years of the Internet. News that old probably never made it to the Web.

What was the first knob on the bureau?

She closed her eyes and tried to remember.

A beaver with a red ribbon around its neck.

She typed "Nebraska cities with beaver in the name" into her phone.

Beaver City, Nebraska, popped up. Population five hundred and eight.

"That is *small*," she murmured to herself.

Charity had something like twenty thousand people. Maybe Kris had worked his way up to larger cities. No doubt he'd honed his skills over the years.

But who would have known about the bureau? The gingerbreads knew he'd hidden things inside it.

His ex-wife had been the obvious suspect, but she never would have sold the furniture to Declan if she knew the treasures were inside it.

Who else would be close enough to him that he might share his secrets? Did he have kids? The will his wife had shared with Declan declared her his only beneficiary, so maybe no kids. Any kids he didn't like enough to leave something to, he probably didn't tell about his hiding spots.

Charlotte slapped her forehead.

The chest of drawers was Christmas-themed. Even the beaver had a red bow around its neck.

She'd been running under the assumption Kris had built the piece, but there was no reason to assume he possessed woodworking skills on that level. *Maybe the chest had been one of the gifts donated.* Maybe a local craftsman had given it to Kris to raffle for charity, and then the con man had walked away with it.

Charlotte heard her own thoughts and laughed.

Charity.

The last town on his list to rob was Charity, Florida.

Was there a more perfect city for a charity con man to rob as his swan song?

If the Pineapple knob had already been made—if he picked his victims based on the knob designs, he must have thought he died and gone to heaven when he found a town called Charity containing a huge community called Pineapple Port.

Her phone buzzed. The front yard camera had been tripped.

Shoot. She'd been getting so much good thinking done in her forced surveillance boredom she'd forgotten about the actual surveillance.

She looked up and spotted Jason walking down the path from his front door to his car. He wore shorts and a polo now. His hair was wet as if he'd just stepped out of the shower. He hopped in his car and pulled out of his driveway.

Thrilled to start her car and get the air conditioning rolling, Charlotte waited and then followed at a safe distance.

The true identities of Kris and the Gingerbreads would have to wait.

CHAPTER TWENTY-TWO

Jason drove out of town toward Tampa. The traffic gave Charlotte plenty of cover as she crept along behind him, dodging behind different cars on and off to keep from always hovering in the same spot in his rearview mirror.

He headed towards Ybor City.

This could be it. Don't turn, don't turn, don't—

Jason veered to the right to take an exit, and she followed.

Shoot.

As traffic thinned, she fell back and followed him into Ybor City.

Jason pulled to a stop, and Charlotte eased into a spot on the corner and put her car into park. She pointed the dash-cam she'd set up to point in Jason's direction and found her phone to check the address of the woman Stephanie didn't want him messing with.

12th Street, Ybor City.

She glanced at the street sign.

12th Street.

It wasn't illegal for Jason to talk to Stephanie's witness. In fact, it was his job. Taking pictures of him talking to her or knocking on her door wouldn't prove a thing. Somehow,

Charlotte had to *prove* he was paying witnesses to lie.

She dug into the backpack she'd brought containing every piece of spy equipment she'd acquired in the last month, feeling a little like a low-rent Batwoman. Finding her binoculars, she pulled them out and trained her attention on the D.A.

Jason knocked on the witness's door. A woman matching the photo Stephanie had sent Charlotte answered. He appeared to introduce himself, and she let him in.

Charlotte hopped out of her car and scurried down the road. She walked past the house and then ducked between it and the one next door. Peering through a bush and into the window, she spotted Jason and the woman sitting on her sofa, talking. The window was cracked open, and she could hear the murmur of their conversation. She pulled out her phone and held it up to videotape and hopefully capture their transaction.

No sooner did she have the camera in place than a dog barked behind her, and she flung herself through the bush, rolling back and away from the sound. The phone skittered across the dirt.

A Rottweiler with a head as large as a pumpkin stared at her from behind the metal fence surrounding the neighbor's yard. Charlotte's heart felt like it was going to pound out of her chest.

The dog stared at her.

She wanted to tell it everything was okay, but with the window cracked, she didn't dare speak. It would be hard to explain what she was doing in the woman's bushes.

She reached for her phone, and the dog barked again.

She froze, and he stopped, panting and staring.

She reached out a few more inches, and he barked.

She stopped, and he stopped.

Charlotte sighed. *Oh, we've got a real funny dog here.*

In one quick movement, she snatched her phone and jumped to her feet to sprint back out to the sidewalk. The dog accompanied her with a soundtrack of low woofs.

Once on the sidewalk, she slowed herself to a stroll, walking as casually as she could with her heart pounding against her ribcage. She tried to look bored, coming just short of whistling. The dog owner peered through her front window to watch her ease by.

Charlotte reached the end of the block and leaned against a street pole there, breathless. She'd been so busy looking innocent that she'd forgotten to breathe. It felt as though the dog had taken a year off her life.

So much for recording Jason.

Even if she'd had the guts to hold her ground, the phone wouldn't have picked up any sound but the dog's barks.

She remained against the pole, trying to decide her next move. Down the block, she spotted Jason leaving the house. He stopped to shake hands and hug the woman before strolling back to his car.

Did he hug everyone he interviewed? The woman obviously trusted him, and his easy stroll said *mission accomplished.*

Jason got in his car and drove past her, making a right to head back home. She turned away to keep him from seeing her face, just in case.

She didn't need to follow him anymore.

Charlotte walked back down the block. She turned on her phone's video and slipped it into the chest pocket of her linen shirt, careful that the camera lens hovered above the edge.

She knocked on the woman's door.

The witness answered, scowling.

"Yes?"

"Rosita?"

"Yes?"

"I think you were just talking to my boss, Jason Walsh?"

The woman's expression softened. "Yes. Very nice man."

"Isn't he? In fact, he's *so* nice, he told me to run back here and offer you a little *more* money."

The woman's eyes lit up. "No. Seriously?"

Charlotte tried not to appear excited.

I think this might just work.

She cleared her throat. "Yep. That's the kind of man he is. He felt like he shortchanged you a little because he didn't have enough cash on him, but I wanted to let you know there's more coming."

The woman pounded her own chest with her fist twice before resting her flattened palm across it. "That's wonderful."

Charlotte grimaced. "Shoot. I forget how much he said he already gave you."

"Five hundred dollars."

"Right. Okay, that makes sense. Because he told me to make it an even thousand."

The woman made a little whooping noise.

"I don't have it with me, but he asked me to go get it and bring it back. I just wanted to make sure you're still going to be here."

"Oh *si, si*. I'll be here."

"Okay. And...wait. Let me make sure I have the right case."

"It's the Edwardo Castillo case. I saw Edwardo the night he was accused. I know he didn't do it."

"But you're not going to say that on the stand."

"No. I'm not going to say that." Rosita looked left and right and leaned forward, her volume dropping low. "He is a terrible boy anyway. He deserves what he gets."

"We agree. Great. That's the right case. Okay. Well, I'll be back."

"Thank you."

"You're welcome. See you in a bit."

Charlotte walked back to her car. Inside, she played back the video on her phone.

She'd captured the entire conversation on tape.

"Whoo hoo!"

Gotcha!

She called Declan.

"I just totally nailed this job," she said when he answered.

"Stephanie's job?"

"Yep. Done and *done*."

"That's great."

"Yep. I just wanted to double check with you before I sent her the evidence she needs. You have the whole fingerprint book, right? All the back pages aren't blank or some such nonsense?"

"No, it seems like a complete book. But I do have some bad news for you. I had some time to kill here and ran through it, comparing the fingerprint you gave me. None matched."

Charlotte nodded. "I'm not surprised. I have a new theory on what happened, and I don't think it had anything to do with Jamie turning Charity into Witness Disney World."

"With a rat instead of a mouse," added Declan.

Charlotte laughed. "Ha! Good one. I wish I'd thought of that."

Declan chuckled. "I think we're back to you owing *me*."

"Fair enough. I'll get dinner tonight for *real*."

"I won't hold my breath."

Charlotte hung up and texted Stephanie to see if she was available. She confirmed she was.

She sent the compressed video file and waited.

Three minutes later, her phone pinged.

"That'll do," was all Stephanie's text said.

"That'll do?" Charlotte said aloud to no one. "How about *thanks*? How about *that's perfect*?"

She knew someone who would appreciate her efforts a little better.

Grumbling to herself, she dialed Frank.

"Frank here."

"Where are you? Are you at home?"

"No, I'm at the office."

"Okay. I'm going to swing by. I have a theory on who killed Kristopher Rudolph I want to bounce off you, and we need to do a license plate check."

"On a black truck?"

Charlotte's brow knit. "Yes. How did you know? Did you talk to Darla about their possum trouble?"

"Possum trouble?"

Charlotte grimaced. *Maybe I wasn't supposed to share that part of the story.*

"The black truck with the Nebraska plate," she answered, hoping Frank wouldn't notice she'd left out any mention of possums.

Frank rattled off the license plate number Tilly had given her. Charlotte was dumbfounded.

"That's the truck's plate number. Darla remembered the plate? Did you talk to Tilly?"

Frank ignored her questions and continued. "Is the guy you think did it named Randy Dobbins?"

"Huh? No. I mean, maybe. I don't know. Is that who owns the truck?"

Frank chuckled. "No. That's who just walked in and confessed."

CHAPTER TWENTY-THREE

One Week Earlier

The four gingerbread men pushed their way into Kris Rudolph's house, tripping over their foam-wrapped feet, doing their best to appear *aggressive*. That had been the game plan. Gingerbread Three came up with it from her days cheerleading.

Be aggressive. Be-Ee aggressive!

Scare him. Confuse him. Keep him off guard. Don't let him talk unless he was telling them what they wanted to know.

Kristopher Rudolph's mouth formed into a ruby, oh, a dash of cherry against his white beard. His pupils ringed with white, and he threw up his hands.

Gingerbread One gave Kris a hard shove that sent him stumbling back until his lounge chair caught the back of his legs, and he collapsed into it.

Kris moved to rise, only to be pushed back into his seat by brown, foamy hands.

"Who are you?"

Gingerbread Two slapped his chest. "We're your worst nightmare."

"The Four Gingerbread Men of the Apocalypse," added Four.

The other three cookies turned to look at Four, and he shrugged.

"What? I just thought of it."

Gingerbread One returned to business. "Tell us where our stuff is. All of it. Since the beginning. Every town. Every item."

Kris scowled. "I don't know what you're talking about."

"Yes, you do. You've scammed your last little town, scumbag," said Three.

"We want it all back. Especially the money," said Two.

Kris pointed toward the door. "Get out of my house before I call the police."

Four laughed. "You? Call the police? Somehow I doubt that."

"Let's take him like we planned," suggested Two. "I don't like doing this here. Too many neighbors."

One held up a mitted hand. "Give him a second to answer."

"Randy's got a point," said Three, the only female voice in the group.

"No names!" shrieked Two.

One glanced at him and put a hand on his shoulder. "Easy."

Three lowered her voice and leaned towards One. "Sorry. But *he* does have a point. This garbageface isn't going to tell us where *everything* is now. We need bank accounts...he could have multiple storage lockers all over the country—"

Four turned to her. "Garbageface?"

She huffed. "I have kids, dog butt."

"Speaking of dogs, that dog won't stop barking," interjected Two, motioning toward the back of the house.

"No, you're right. We should maybe take him." One pulled off the head of his costume and wriggled out of it to the waist to free his hands.

"He can see your face," hissed Two.

One shrugged. "It don't matter. What's he going to do? Call the cops on us and blow his whole operation?" He took a bag from Four's mitt and pulled a fifth gingerbread man suit from it.

"Hold out his legs," he said.

The others pounced on Kris to hold out his limbs.

He grunted, struggling to resist. "What are you doing?"

The others forced him into the costume, pushing and jerking his body up and down, left and right, until he'd donned it.

"He looks heavier than I remember," said Three.

Kris pulled one hand free and slapped at his captors. "You people are insane if you think I'm going to let you carry me out of here."

Four wrestled to regain control of the slapping hand.

"Oh, you're *going* to let us," said One, pulling up his own costume.

Four grabbed Kris's arm, and the old man lurched forward. "Help!"

"*Dangit.*" Four slapped his padded hand over Kris's mouth to muffle the screams. Kris lifted his hips, his arms still pinned.

"I got it," said Two, grabbing a cloth elf from where it sat perched on the edge of the television table. He brushed Four's mitt from Kris's face and shoved the elf into Kris's mouth, and held it there. The screams stopped, but Kris began to buck as if he was being electrocuted.

"See? Quiet as a mouse," said Two. "Hold still, you fat bastard."

Four pressed on Kris's shoulders, holding him as still as he could. Kris shook his head back and forth as Two struggled to hold the elf in place.

"Put the head on him," suggested Three.

With Two still holding the elf against his mouth, One picked up the spare head and set it over Kris's skull. Kris fell still.

Three put her mitts on her hips. "Wow. That worked even better than I thought. It works with horses. Put on the blinders, and they calm right down."

"See, isn't it better when you don't fight us?" asked One, rapping Kris on the top of his foam head with his mitt.

Four chuckled. "He's like a little kid. You just have to tire him out."

Two released the elf and pulled his hand out from under the head, holding out his fingers as if Kris were a Jenga about to topple.

Kris remained still. No neighbors' lights switched on. It seemed the worst had ended. The group released a collective sigh.

"We need to look for that chest of drawers," suggested Three, wandering towards the back. "I know he had you build it for a reason."

One nodded his giant foam head, following her. "Old man Farkus and I spent three months working on that thing. It's his masterpiece."

"Found it!" called Three from the back of the house. "It's *really* heavy, though."

Two looked at Four. "How do you think we should do this?"

"The dog's back here locked in the bathroom. A little thing," called Three.

"With a big mouth," said Two.

"I'm sure he stole it." One slid past Three as she peeked in on the dog and reentered the living room. "Kris is calm now. Let's take him to the car and away from here, and we'll come back for the bureau."

Two huffed. "Can't we just take it all now? Won't people get suspicious if we come back? Maybe they'll let us slide the first time, thinking we're part of Kris's festivities, but twice—"

Three returned to the living room and cut Two short. "We'll need all four of us to lift that bureau into the truck. And we can't leave him unattended anywhere."

One waved a mitt in the air. "We don't need to take it. We just need to open it and see what he has inside and take back *that*. There's no point taking the whole thing."

From the back of the house, the dog continued his steady yap.

"Doesn't Farkus want his furniture back?" asked Four.

"Farkus died last year."

"Hey guys," interjected Two.

"But you know how to get into it?" asked Four, ignoring Two and continuing his conversation.

"Yeah. I helped him build it, remember?"

"Guys?" repeated Two.

One turned. "What?"

Two pointed at Kris's still body with a mitted hand. "It doesn't look like he's breathing."

"What?"

All four gingerbread faces turned to Kris. Two removed his head and one mitt and pulled the foam head off Kris.

The tinge of blue circling Kristopher Rudolph's lips didn't look *right*. His eyes were wide and still.

And *open*.

Three gasped. "He's dead?"

Two covered his mouth with his free hand, and the four of them gawped at the toy elf staring back at them from beneath Kris's mustache.

"He must have had a heart attack," said Two.

One turned. "A heart attack? Is it just me, or is there an elf sticking out of his mouth?"

Four leaned in for a better look at the little face staring back at him. "It looks like he suffocated. Where's the rest of the elf?"

"What do you mean?" asked Two, his voice dropping to a whisper.

"Did you stuff an elf down his throat?" asked Three.

Two dropped the hand from his mouth and gaped. "No, I just pressed it *against* his mouth."

One leaned close. A single white-gloved hand poked from the corner of Kris's lips as if the elf was trying to climb out.

"The legs," he muttered.

"What?" asked Two.

"The legs. He must have sucked down those long legs and choked."

Two put his hands on his head. "No. No, no, no, *no*...This isn't happening. I didn't kill him."

"What are we going to do now?" asked Four.

"Do we still open up the chest?" asked Three.

"Who cares about the chest now?" screeched Two.

Four shrugged. "Well, it's *done* now. We might as well take our time and get what we can. We don't have to worry about him starting to scream."

"Can we cover his face or something?" asked Three. She picked up the gingerbread man's head and slipped it back over Kris's.

Two gaped at Kris's motionless form, his hands on his cheeks, doing his best imitation of Munch's *The Scream* if the tortured soul in that famous painting happened to be wearing the body of a gingerbread man costume. His bare hand dragged down the skin of his cheek, distorting his expression on one side.

He turned to the others. "What are you talking about? We can't stay here. *I killed a man.* What am I going to *do*?"

Three patted him on the shoulder. "I don't think anyone should die, but if anyone deserved it, it was this piece of dog poop—"

"Let's go look at the chest and get out of here," said One.

Two flopped into the stuffed chair across from Kris. "What am I going to do?" he asked no one in particular.

The others watched him mumble the phrase over and over to himself until One broke the spell.

"*Chest.* Let's go."

"Leave him," said Four. He patted Two on the head. "We'll be back in a sec. You stay here. Take it easy."

One, Three, and Four marched toward the back of the house. They pulled the chest of drawers away from the wall, and then One returned to the front room in search of tools. "Randy, we're going to need some tools. At least a Phillips-head screwdriver. Help me look—" He stopped in his tracks. The front room appeared *smoky*. Through the haze, he spotted Two crouched at the bottom of the Christmas tree.

"What are you doing?"

"I'm burning the evidence."

Flames rose from the packages beneath the tree, and Two stumbled back, grabbing for the head of his nearby costume to keep it from burning.

One raised his arms. "Are you crazy?"

Two whirled on him, his eyes wild. "*We have to burn the evidence.* We have to make it look like an accident."

"You lit the tree on fire while we're in the back of the house wearing a flammable costume? Have you lost your mind?"

Two rubbed at his face. "I can't go to jail. I have a *family*."

"We all have families, you jackass!"

The flames grew higher.

One turned and ran back down the hall.

"Everyone out!"

Three and Four looked up at him from their position around the bureau. "Why?"

"Randy's burning down the house."

"What?"

"He thinks he's covering evidence, and he's burning down the house. We have to get out of here."

"But we haven't opened the chest yet," said Four.

"Do you want to burn to death in a gingerbread man costume? Get out of the house! Now!"

Three and Four straightened to follow One as he galloped down the hallway.

Three stopped at the bathroom door. "The dog!"

She opened the door and snatched the pet into her arms before heading for the front door. The animal's thin red leash dragged behind her as she ran.

The front room had filled with smoke. Flames raged beneath the tree, consuming the packages and licking at the leg of Kris's costume as the four gingerbreads burst out of the house.

Two struggled to put his head back on as they ran for the car. Three stopped at the curb.

"What are you doing?" asked Four, pausing as the other two flopped foamy feet toward the vehicle, their legs cocked out at stiff, unnatural angles as they ran.

"The dog. It belongs to someone here. You know how he works."

Three used the leash to tie the tiny dog to the white lamppost sitting curbside of Kris's house.

"They'll find it here."

Four tried to grab her arm as best he could with his cookie mitt. "Great, let's go."

They scrambled to the truck and wrestled their bulky bodies inside, peeling off just as one of the neighbors appeared at their window, staring at the flickering glow in Kris's living room.

CHAPTER TWENTY-FOUR

Charlotte pulled into the sheriff's office parking lot and sprang out of her car to run inside. The reception area sat empty except for Linda's goldfish that silently circled its bowl.

"Frank?" she called.

"In here."

Charlotte jogged down the hall and popped her head into Frank's office. He sat behind his desk, facing a man sitting in the chair she usually occupied when visiting. The man twisted to look at her. She didn't recognize him.

"She was at the pawn shop," he said to Frank before turning his attention back to her. "Sorry about that."

She scowled before realizing what he meant. "You were one of the gingerbreads?"

The man's expression darkened. "Twenty years as a master electrician, father of two, local bowling champion—and now I'll be remembered as a *gingerbread man* for the rest of my life."

"You're someone Kris cheated," she said, sitting in another chair against the wall.

He nodded.

"Randy Dobbins here just told me the whole story of how he accidentally killed Kris trying to shut him up with an elf."

"It was an accident?" asked Charlotte.

Randy nodded. "Absolutely."

"And you tried to set the house on fire to hide your mistake?"

He nodded again. "I panicked. It was stupid."

"But you saved the dog."

Randy sighed. "Maybe they'll shave off a few years for that."

Frank tilted back in his chair. "I was telling Mr. Dobbins here that there's one problem with his story."

"What's that?"

"He said he worked alone."

Charlotte shook her head. "There were *three* gingerbread men at the store. And there may be a fourth. A woman."

Frank nodded and raised a piece of paper from his desk. "And then there's the little issue of the truck he arrived in being owned by a Carl Stussy."

Randy looked away and shrugged. "I borrowed the truck."

"Are you from Beaver City, Nebraska, by any chance?" asked Charlotte.

Frank laughed, and Charlotte looked at him. "What are you laughing about?"

"Randy isn't, but Carl is. How'd you know that?"

"I was *right*." Charlotte shook her fist in the air to celebrate. "Did the owner of the truck build the chest of drawers?"

Randy's cheek twitched. "I worked alone."

"Are you saying the other two gingerbreads are robots?"

"I don't know what you're talking about."

"You just said you remembered me from the pawn shop, and there were three gingerbreads."

Randy made a grunting noise. "I don't know what you mean."

Charlotte sighed and sat back in her chair. "It's nice of you to try and cover for your friends. They didn't have anything to do with Kris's death after all. Right?"

Randy glanced at her and then looked at Frank. "Shouldn't you take me to jail or something?"

A voice called from the reception area.

"Hello?"

Frank stood and pulled his cuffs from his belt. He cuffed Randy to the chair.

"Keep an eye on him," he said, walking into the hall.

Randy's eyes flicked in the direction of the hallway, and Charlotte thought he appeared more nervous than he had a moment before. She heard voices and stood to peer into the reception area. Two men, one older and one a middle-aged redhead, stood with a brown-haired woman talking with Frank. The sheriff motioned for them to follow him down the hall, and Charlotte ducked back to her seat. She looked up as they entered as if she had no idea they were on their way.

"I believe you all know Randy Dobbins," said Frank, making his way back to his chair.

"I don't know who these people are," mumbled Randy, refusing to look.

The smaller, red-headed man put his hand on Randy's shoulder. "We couldn't let you do it. We couldn't let you take all the blame."

The gray-haired, mustachioed man nodded in agreement. "Coming here to teach him a lesson was my crackpot idea."

"I started the Facebook page," added the woman.

Charlotte perked. "The Facebook page?"

"Victims of the Christmas Con Man."

"There's a Facebook page for people Kristopher Rudolph conned?"

The three newcomers nodded.

"Yeah, though he wasn't Kris when I met him. My town knew him as Jack Jingle," said the redhead.

Frank waved his hands in the air. "Hold on, hold on. Let me get all of your names first."

He picked up a pen and started writing. "I've got Randy Dobbins of Lemons, Missouri."

"The lemon was somewhere near the middle on the right," said Charlotte, remembering the lemon-shaped knob on the chest of drawers.

"Carl Timchell of Beaver City, Nebraska."

The gray-haired man raised his hand.

"Ah, you're Beaver City. First place hit," said Charlotte.

"It was. Lucky me," said Carl.

"Thirty years ago? Are you the one who knew about the bureau?"

"I helped build it. Friend of mine, Joe Farkus, was the true craftsman. It was his pride and joy. Never guessed why Kringle asked him to make it—though we figured it out fast enough when he disappeared on Christmas with fifteen thousand dollars of our hard-earned cash and a list of donated items that would break your heart."

"His name was Kringle, then?"

"Kris Kringle. Year one, he didn't have to get so creative."

"Think he was from nearby?"

"Probably. Who knows if anything he ever said was true. He showed up in June and left us in December."

"Same as everyone," said the woman.

Charlotte's head filled with more questions. "Did—"

"Hold on," barked Frank. "I'm not done with roll call."

"Sorry."

"Okay, we got Randy, Carl...that means you're...?" Frank turned to the redhead.

"Cole Harper from Rising Fawn, Georgia."

"Ah, I thought that was a *rein*deer knob. I bet it was a deer," mumbled Charlotte.

Frank eyeballed Charlotte and pantomimed zipping his lips.

"Sorry," she mumbled from the side of her mouth as if the other side had already been zipped.

Frank read his notepad and looked up. "Which leaves us with you."

The woman nodded as he motioned to her. "Karen Hatchett of Hot Coffee, Mississippi."

Charlotte laughed out loud. "Hot Coffee?"

Karen nodded. "Third row down, fourth knob in. The fancy china coffee cup—not that there's anything fancy about Hot Coffee."

"So you all met through the Facebook page?"

Carl nodded. "I suggested we come and get him when Karen found a mention of Pineapple Port online."

Cole interrupted. "Carl knew the last knob on the chest was a pineapple, but we'd lost hope when no one in Pine Apple, Alabama, knew anything about a Christmas charity."

"Then I saw a thing online about a big shootout at an old folks' disco down here. It mentioned the lady who owned the place lived in *Pineapple* Port," said Karen.

Charlotte gaped. She knew all about that shootout to which Karen referred—she'd been involved.

Carl picked up the story. "I made a few phone calls, found out he was here and knew he was ready to rob you all blind."

Frank grimaced. "Why didn't you come to me?"

"You don't know how tricky he was. We wanted proof. We wanted to make him admit it on tape," said Karen.

"By torturing him?"

Karen scowled. "No. We were just going to scare him. We certainly didn't mean—"

"*I* didn't mean to kill him," said Randy, finishing his sentence with a great sigh of what sounded like relief.

Frank cocked an eyebrow. "You just stuffed the elf in his mouth—"

A flash of anger crossed Randy's face. "To shut him *up*. I didn't realize the legs—"

"And the fire? Was that an accident?"

"I told you. I panicked."

Charlotte leaned forward. "The thing I can't understand is why you stayed in town. Why didn't you go back to your homes where you'd probably never have been found?"

"That's my fault too," said Carl. "I wanted the stuff in that chest of drawers back. I was going to give it back to the people he robbed. I hoped maybe we'd find a little money I could give Farkus's widow. It would have been something. Figured maybe there was a little something left for each town he robbed."

Frank stood and put his hands on his hips. "Well, the good news is there *was* something in each of those hidden drawers."

Karen's eyes lit up. "There was?"

"Yep." Frank sighed. "The bad news is I'm going to have to arrest you all for murder."

CHAPTER TWENTY-FIVE

"I'm going to kill him."

Stephanie weighed the pros and cons of confronting Jason with the video Charlotte sent her. She had to admit Declan's little angel had done her job. The evidence was undeniable. She could present it to Jason and have something to hold over him forever...or she could take it to the judge and ruin his career.

Tough call.

She idly spun her phone on her desk, deliberating. The phone chimed, and she stopped it.

A text from Jason.

Speak of the devil.

She lifted the phone and read the message.

We need to talk. Meet me at the abandoned rug warehouse. Fifteen minutes.

Stephanie frowned. She knew the building he meant. She drove by it every day. The enormous metal warehouse had been abandoned after its owner went bankrupt. It wasn't the sort of spot people held business meetings in.

Why would Jason want to meet her in an abandoned warehouse? Why the cloak and dagger?

She smiled.

He knows.

He must have seen Charlotte talking to the witness after he left. He put two and two together and figured *she* was pulling the strings. Now he was coming crawling, begging her not to ruin him, in a location she couldn't possibly have rigged with sound or cameras in time to capture their meeting.

Oh, I like this.

It would be fun to hear him beg.

She texted him back.

See you soon.

She grabbed her purse and drove the mile and a half to the warehouse, running through the things she might want to ask for in return for her mercy.

I might never lose another case again.

She pulled into the parking lot. Weeds sprouted from every fissure in the blacktop. She stepped out of her car to head towards the front door, doing her best to keep the rocks from tearing the leather from her heels.

The entrance had been left cracked open.

Stephanie patted her soft-bodied purse and felt for her gun inside. Jason was a rich-kid dirtball, but he didn't seem like the kind of person who would draw her to an abandoned warehouse to kill her.

Still... it didn't hurt to be safe.

Heaven help him if he does try something.

He has no idea who he's messing with.

She passed Jason's car and glanced inside. No one was hiding in the back. If he'd brought backup, they were inside with him.

Stephanie pushed open the door and walked inside. The only light filtered through rusted holes in the ceiling, shining to the floor like lasers, dust swirling in their centers.

She squinted, allowing her eyes to adjust to the dim light.

"Hello?"

As her vision improved, she spotted several large rolls of carpet piled in the far corner of the room. Beside them sat a man in a chair.

"Jason?"

Something was wrong with his position. He looked awkward. *Slumpy.*

Why is he just sitting there?

Something moved in the murky darkness behind the man in the chair. A hand appeared, almost ghostly, glowing as it entered a thin beam of light to Jason's left.

The hand wasn't empty.

Stephanie saw the flash of a gun. Bolting to the right, she scrambled to find the weapon in her bag, pulling it as a shot echoed through the tin can of a building. She lunged sideways and fired into the dark corner, landing hard on her shoulder.

Her head hit something hard, and the world went black.

Stephanie reached up, her fingers touching something rough and crunchy. She opened her eyes.

Carpet.

Her fingers recoiled from the rug. She coughed and sat up, hand rising to touch the tender spot on the side of her head. She looked at her fingers and found them red with blood.

Ow.

She remembered rolling behind the stacks of carpet. Dove there.

Why did I dive—?

There was a gunshot.

Looking to her left, she spotted her gun lying on the ground.

I'm alive. That's a step in the right direction.

She peeked from behind her hiding place, careful not to touch the dusty carpet again.

A man, sitting in a chair.

She remembered it now.

Jason.

She'd had trouble seeing him before. She remembered being unsure it was him. Now a beam of light that hadn't been there before illuminated his features.

Where did that come from?

She glanced up at the source. A new hole in the roof.

Bullet-sized.

"Jason?"

No answer.

Stephanie pulled herself to her feet and retrieved her weapon.

Had she imagined the other person? Was it Jason who'd shot at her?

Holding her gun in front of her, she moved toward him.

"Don't do this," she warned, creeping towards him. "I don't know if you think you're being funny or threatening, but I can't tell you how close you are to being dead."

Something about Jason's expression had bothered her since the moment she peeked from behind the rolled carpet. As she grew closer, she realized what it was.

Jason's eyes were wide open.

Unblinking.

"Jason?"

She pointed the gun to the ceiling and reached out to feel his neck for a pulse.

His skin felt cold to the touch.

Behind her, someone called her name, and she whirled, ready   to   fire.

CHAPTER TWENTY-SIX

The four gingerbreads, sans costumes, walked to Frank's holding cell without complaint. He made the necessary calls to have them transferred for processing while Charlotte waited anxiously for him to finish his official business.

"What do you think is going to happen to them?" she asked when he returned to his office, looking grim.

"It's a tough call. There are some extenuating circumstances. The other three might get away with almost no time. The one who put the elf in the man's mouth could get as little as a year for manslaughter. It depends if his lawyer can get some sympathy."

"It doesn't sound like it will be hard to convince people Kris had it coming."

Frank sighed. "Murder's still murder."

Charlotte's phone buzzed, and she glanced at it, expecting it to be Declan.

Stephanie.

Charlotte groaned.

Please don't tell me she's decided I didn't do enough.

Gathering evidence on Jason *had* felt too easy.

She read the text.

Come quick. Empty carpet warehouse. NOW.

She scowled. "That's weird."

"What's that?"

"It's a text from Stephanie."

"You guys really are buddies now. Having a sleepover tonight?"

"Very funny."

"I liked it when you had friends sleep over as a kid because Bob would always ask me to go bowling with him to get the hell out of the house."

Charlotte chuckled at the memory. "Mariska always insisted she chaperone my sleepovers when I had a *whole house* to myself across the street. It didn't seem fair."

Frank nodded. "Didn't seem fair to Bob either."

Charlotte returned her attention to her phone. "She wants me to come to the empty rug warehouse."

"That big rusty metal building?"

Charlotte nodded. "Says it's urgent."

"No idea what it's about?"

"None."

"Well, I think we've got Kris's murder all wrapped up and the cookies in the oven. There's nothing left for you to do here if you want to go."

Charlotte sighed. "I don't know that I *want* to go."

Frank shrugged. "Maybe she needs your help. You were just helping her with something, weren't you?"

"Yes." Charlotte typed *see you there* into her phone. "Fine. I'll go. Like you said, maybe she needs my help again. At least it would be a paycheck. I guess you know where I'm going if something happens."

"What does that mean?"

Charlotte frowned, unsure she wanted to underline for Frank just how dangerous Stephanie could be. "Nothing. I'll see you later."

Frank held out a hand. "Case is over. I need that badge back."

"Gotta go, bye!"

Charlotte scooted out the door before he could ask for the badge a second time.

That was close.

She headed outside and started the air conditioning in the Volvo before calling Declan.

"You don't know anything going on with Stephanie right now, do you?" she asked.

"You mean in general? Do you have a few hours?"

"No. I mean, right *now*. She just texted me and asked me to come to the abandoned rug warehouse."

"What? Why?"

"I don't know. That's why I thought I'd check with you."

Declan clucked his tongue. "I don't like the sound of that."

"Me neither. So I figured it wouldn't hurt to have you know where I'm going, just in case."

"Maybe I should come too."

"Nah. Just be sure they check her bathtub for my blood after she chops me into bits and feeds me to the alligators. Have the cops use Luminal. I'll try and bleed a lot so you can catch her. Place will light up like a Christmas tree—"

"That's not even funny."

Charlotte laughed. "Sorry. I'm kidding. She isn't going to kill me. I'm pretty sure if she planned to, she would have done it by now."

Declan grunted. "Give me a call as soon as you know what's going on."

"I will."

"And Charlotte...don't trust her."

"Duh."

"I mean it. Don't put anything past her."

"I'll be fine."

Charlotte disconnected and tossed her phone on the passenger seat to drive to the abandoned warehouse.

Two cars and several metric gallons of weeds and crumbling blacktop graced the large parking lot of the carpet warehouse. Stephanie's candy apple-red viper she recognized. The other car looked like the blue Audi she'd followed earlier. Jason Walsh's.

She's not going to let him confront me, is she? Pretend she didn't know anything about me following him and interviewing his bribery victim?

Charlotte shook her head. It didn't make sense. Even if Stephanie was going to play dumb and let her private eye take the heat, why would she hold the meeting in an abandoned warehouse?

Charlotte closed the door and let her gaze sweep across the neglected landscape. A lizard scooting across the pavement as she neared the front door proved the only sign of life.

The only set of windows on the front of the building had been boarded over.

The door hung on crooked hinges.

Ajar.

It looked as though the chain that had once held it shut had been snipped by bolt cutters.

She's really going to the ends of the earth to pick a weird meeting spot.

Charlotte pushed open the door with her fingertips and stepped inside.

The light played tricks on her eyes, the room dim but for beams of light shooting through the roof to the ground. One of the beams stabbed at the back of a woman who looked like Stephanie from behind. Her back was bent as if she was crouched over something in the corner.

"Stephanie?"

The woman whirled, a gun in her hand.

Charlotte's hands shot into the air, lowering slightly once she confirmed the woman was Stephanie. "Whoa, it's *me*."

Stephanie's eyes squinted. "What are you doing here?"

"You texted me."

"I what?"

"I just got a message from you telling me to come here." She looked past Stephanie to what looked like a man sitting in a chair. Something about him seemed off.

"Is that Jason?"

Stephanie stepped in front of the man as if to block her view and remained still, staring at Charlotte, the gun pointed in her direction.

Charlotte huffed. "Could you put down the gun now?"

Stephanie lowered the weapon to her side. Her shoulders slumped. The air of confidence that seemed to follow Declan's ex like a halo had dissipated. The blonde bent down to grab a purse next to her and rifled through it.

"My phone's gone."

Charlotte lowered her hands.

"You didn't text me?"

"No."

Charlotte took a step forward. "Is that Jason Walsh?"

Stephanie nodded. "He asked me to come here."

"Is he okay? He seems kind of...*still*."

Stephanie took a step to the side and motioned to him with the gun. "He's dead."

Charlotte felt her nerves vibrate, scared to ask the question filling the space between them like a living thing.

"Should I ask?" was the best she could muster, her toe dragging toward the door behind her in case she needed to bolt.

Stephanie shook her head. "I didn't kill him. I told you—he asked me to come here."

"Those two things aren't mutually exclusive."

"He was like this when I got here."

"Did he text you?"

"Yes." Stephanie squinted one eye at her. "Why?"

"You texted me, remember?"

"But I didn't."

"Exactly."

Stephanie nodded slowly as if in thought. To Charlotte, she seemed a step slower than usual.

Stephanie shrugged. "Right. Anyway, I walked inside, and he was sitting in this chair. There was a gun, and then—" She shook her head. "I can't remember. I returned fire and dove. Hit my head."

"You fired?"

"Yes. He...someone fired at me."

"He shot? I thought you said he was dead when you got here."

Stephanie grimaced and gingerly touched her head as if she was in pain. "I said he was *like this*. I think he was dead."

"But you shot at him?"

"I wasn't aiming at *him*."

"That doesn't mean you didn't hit him."

Stephanie snorted a laugh. "Yes, it does."

"Are you sure he's dead now? We need to call an ambulance."

Again, Stephanie touched her free hand to the side of her head. Even in the dim light, Charlotte could see the blood on her fingertips.

"You're hurt. Are *you* shot?"

"I told you. I hit my head on the floor."

Stephanie stepped forward as if trying to catch her balance. She raised the gun again, her hand shaking. "I'm going. Back off."

"You're not going anywhere. You're hurt, and you may have just killed a man."

"I didn't. I'm good. I can be good." She trailed off into a mumble.

Charlotte scowled. "What does that mean?"

Stephanie's expression hardened. She trained the wavering gun on Charlotte.

Charlotte heard the gun click.

CHAPTER TWENTY-SEVEN

Charlotte jumped back, hands shooting into the air once more. "Did you just try to *shoot* me?"

Stephanie glanced at the gun. "No. I don't think so." She walked toward Charlotte, gun still raised.

Stephanie's gun clicked a second time.

Charlotte covered her face with her forearms as if she were Wonder Woman, capable of deflecting bullets with magic bracelets. "Are you insane?"

Stephanie opened her gun and, seemingly disgusted, threw her weapon behind her. It clattered across the cement floor.

Stephanie kicked off her heels and marched towards Charlotte. The action stunned Charlotte into inaction. She'd never seen Stephanie remove her heels before. She thought the woman slept in them.

That has to be a bad sign.

It was now or never.

Now.

Charlotte bolted forward. She had a muddled plan to tackle Stephanie and subdue her. She wasn't sure what she'd do after that, but it was better than standing like a dope while her arch-nemesis shot an empty gun at her.

Stephanie's body twisted, and her foot appeared where her *hands* had been a moment earlier, arcing through the air. Before

Charlotte could put together what happened, she felt the side of Stephanie's bare foot glance her shoulder as she dodged to keep it from catching her in the jaw.

What was that?

Again Charlotte tried to grab the blonde, only to find herself blocking punches with sweeps of her arms. As quickly as it had all begun, Stephanie disengaged and bolted for the door. Charlotte lunged to grab the back of her jacket, hooking it with a finger. The fabric ripped as Stephanie's momentum jerked her forward. Charlotte used the resulting forward stumble to launch into a tackle, clipping the back of Stephanie's heels and felling her.

Charlotte crawled up Stephanie's body, scaling her like a mountain climber. Stephanie flipped, roaring, and the women rolled across the cement, wrestling for control. With each revolution, Charlotte felt the skin scraping from her elbows and knees. The more they fought, the more lucid Stephanie seemed to become. Her previous dazed, almost childlike expression had contorted into the furious snarl of a caged animal. Charlotte tried not to worry, but she could tell her size, and Stephanie's head injury were the only advantages she possessed against the trained soldier. If Stephanie managed to clear her head and fight with the true skills she obviously possessed...

"Why are you so big?" Stephanie spat as they exchanged glancing blows.

"Why are you so *awful*?" Charlotte grunted back at her.

Charlotte thought she had her foe pinned when Stephanie contorted her back at what seemed like an unnatural angle and wrapped her legs around Charlotte's waist. Stephanie twisted, leverage seeming to come from nowhere, wrenching Charlotte off of her.

Is she made out of rubber?

The back of Charlotte's head hit the floor and the world popped with light as if someone had set off a flashbulb.

No wonder Stephanie seemed dazed. This hurts.

Stephanie's fist connected with her eye. The blonde tornado had mounted her middle with the apparent intention of pummeling her face into a pulp.

Reeling, Charlotte made a rigid line with her right hand and poked out. She felt her fingers sink into Stephanie's gut and heard a breathy groan. Another fist crashed into her cheekbone. Charlotte pulled her feet towards her, preparing to pelvic-thrust Stephanie off of her like a bucking bronco when a voice echoed through the warehouse.

"Stop!"

Charlotte heard footsteps approaching but couldn't see who it was, thanks to both her angle on the floor and the fact her left eye was busy swelling shut.

"Get off of her."

"You're not going to shoot me," said Stephanie, still sounding winded from the fight.

"Don't make me."

Declan.

Charlotte recognized the voice now.

Why had it taken so long to recognize him?

She suspected the clunk on her head had muddled her more than she knew.

She half-rolled and half-crawled out from under Stephanie's straddled legs with no resistance. Skull throbbing, she remained on her hands and knees, head hanging down as she waited for the little hunchback in her brain to stop bouncing up and down on her bells.

"Are you okay?" asked Declan. It sounded as if he was underwater.

"Yes. No. I'm not sure. Probably."

Through her good eye, she saw Declan's feet appear and felt his hand on her arm as he helped her to her feet. He still trained his gun on Stephanie.

Declan steadied her. "Call Frank if you can."

Charlotte felt for her phone and came up empty. Declan handed her his, and she called Frank as instructed, happy to have someone else do the thinking for a moment. Fumbling with the buttons, it took three tries to get the numbers right. Her hands shook with adrenaline.

Finally, she heard Frank's voice.

"Frank here."

Her brain wasn't sure what to say, but her mouth seemed to have no problem. "Come to the warehouse. Now. Bring a gun."

She heard him hit his car sirens, and she hung up.

Stephanie remained sitting on the floor, staring up at them. Her lovely cream suit jacket and skirt were covered in dirt and jagged tears. Even in that state of disarray, Charlotte could tell it cost more than anything she owned.

She glanced at Declan's gun, and it reminded her of Stephanie's clicking weapon.

She grunted.

I think she tried to shoot me. Her suit deserves everything it got.

"What?" asked Declan, hearing her humpf of disapproval.

"She has a gun."

"Where?"

"Over there." Charlotte motioned behind Stephanie as her gaze drifted back to the weapon in Declan's hand.

Wait. When did he get a gun?

"Is that licensed?" she asked. She didn't know why. The words had just come out of her mouth.

Declan frowned, his eyes still trained on the area behind Stephanie. "My gun? Yes. Who is that?"

He pointed to Jason with his eyes, and Charlotte's own orbs widened. She'd almost forgotten about the man in the corner. She took an unsteady step in Jason's direction, careful to give Stephanie a wide berth.

Declan barked. "Charlotte, *no*. We don't know who he is."

She shook her head and continued forward. "We do. It's Assistant District Attorney Jason Walsh."

The body had fallen from the chair and lay in a fetal position, his back to her. Charlotte rolled him over to find wide, glassy eyes staring back at her. She didn't have to be a coroner to know he was very much dead.

"He's dead," she called back to Declan.

"Are you sure?"

"The bullet hole in the center of his head is a dead giveaway." She'd been too far away to notice the wound before, partially hidden beneath his floppy brown hair.

She wandered back to Declan, his mouth a hard line, his jaw flexing as his teeth gritted. In other circumstances, she would have said he looked unbearably sexy, probably even more so if she could see him with both eyes.

Stephanie rose to her feet. Her lip shone bright red where Charlotte had connected during their tussle. Her tongue searched out the blood, and she wiped her mouth with the back of her hand.

Charlotte had never seen her hair in such a mess. It delighted her to no end.

No heels, messy hair, probably going to jail for murder...this is a banner day.

"I'm going," Stephanie said, smoothing her skirt.

Declan shook his head. "You're not."

She swept a hand toward Jason's body, pointing. "I didn't do that."

"Then you won't mind telling the sheriff who did."

"I'm going. I won't be able to figure this out from jail. You'll have to shoot me."

Declan's jaw flexed again. "Don't push me."

Stephanie started walking towards the door, and Declan shot into the air. Both women ducked, throwing their hands over their heads.

"Freeze!" screamed another voice as the reverberation of the gunfire faded. Frank stood in the doorway, his gun drawn. "All of you."

Declan held up his hands. "Frank, it's Declan."

"Right now, I don't care who you are. Put down the gun."

Declan lowered the weapon to the ground and kicked it away from them.

Charlotte glanced at Stephanie. "It's not him, Frank, it's Stephanie. She killed Jason Walsh."

Stephanie glared. "I *didn't*."

"And she shot at me. *Twice*." She turned to Declan. "Seriously. She fired, but she was out of bullets."

Declan grimaced and glared at Stephanie, who shook her head and looked away.

"Exaggeration," she mumbled.

"We'll get it all sorted out." Frank walked forward.

"No. Wait," said Declan, motioning for Frank to stop. "Let me grab her."

Frank scowled. "What?"

"She's trained. She could have that gun out of your hand before you knew what happened."

Frank frowned and looked at Charlotte.

She shrugged. "He's probably right. It couldn't hurt."

Frank sighed. "As a younger man, I'd have smacked your face for suggesting that."

Declan nodded. "I know. But I'm telling you, this isn't about your age. She's dangerous."

Frank motioned to Stephanie with his gun. "Go ahead."

Declan lowered his hands and moved to Stephanie, who seemed to deflate like a balloon as he approached.

"Declan, *don't*," she said, her head shaking back and forth. "Don't. I can't fix things in jail. I have to be out here. I didn't do it. I really don't think I did—"

"If you're innocent, we'll get it sorted."

Stephanie covered her face with her hands. "You don't understand. I'm being set up."

Declan grasped one of Stephanie's wrists and, springing like a trap at his touch, she swung at him with her opposite hand. He blocked it easily and grabbed that wrist as well. In a flash, he had both her arms pinned behind her back.

"No, no, *no!*" her voice rose to a shriek as Frank approached, cuffs in hand.

Her expression shifted from panic to pure hatred as her eyes locked with Charlotte's.

"You're going to *die*," she said, spitting blood to the ground.

"You're going to jail," said Frank, locking the cuffs on her.

Charlotte heard tires sliding along gravel outside. A second later, Deputy Daniel appeared in the doorway, his gun drawn.

"I came as fast as I could, Frank."

"Radio in an ambulance and the coroner's van, and help me get this one to the car."

Frank walked Stephanie out of the building, her chin now held high and defiant. She moved with such purposeful grace it was almost hard to tell who was leading whom.

Declan moved to Charlotte, lightly touching the area around her eye with his thumb. She winced.

"Don't take this the wrong way, but you don't look so good," he murmured.

She leaned into his body to rest her good cheek against him and closed her eyes as he wrapped his arms around her.

"I need karate lessons," she mumbled.

CHAPTER TWENTY-EIGHT

Declan and Charlotte parked in front of The Anne Bonny and braced themselves to enter Seamus's holiday party. Charlotte had insisted on driving. The thrill of having her own car hadn't yet passed.

She was about to open her car door to exit when Declan touched her shoulder.

"Wait a second."

She turned. "Oh no. Did Seamus set up something crazy you need to warn me about?"

He shook his head and slipped his hand in the pocket of his linen shorts to retrieve something she couldn't make out.

"What is it?" she asked.

He held out a small box. "It's for you."

"Christmas isn't for another week."

He shrugged. "I'll have more for you then."

Charlotte tried not to wince. She still hadn't thought of anything to get Declan, and now he had *so many* gifts for her he'd started giving them early.

So much pressure.

She looked at the box. "You want me to open it now? You're sure?"

"I'm sure."

Taking the gift, she pulled the bow on the little box and

unwrapped the paper. Lifting the lid, she revealed two silver pineapples. She recognized them as the ones she'd seen at Jimmy the Jeweler's.

She gaped at him, stunned. "Pineapple earrings! I saw these the other day at Jimmy's and wished they were mine. How did you know?"

Declan shrugged. "Just lucky, I guess. I saw them, and they seemed like you."

She unhooked one from its backing before realizing she was already wearing earrings. She fumbled to remove the jewelry currently in her ears. As she did, she dropped the pineapple earring, and it slipped between the seat and the center console of the car.

"Oh *no*."

"That was fast, even for you," said Declan, sounding amused.

"No, I'll get it. Hold on—"

Charlotte threw open her door and squatted to search under her seat. She lit the flashlight on her phone to illuminate the crevices until the light bounced off the rogue earring. Her body flooded with relief.

"I see it," she announced. She reached under the seat and managed to flick the earring from its nook into a spot where she could grab it.

"Got it!"

She was about to stand when something else under the Volvo's seat caught her eye.

Something vaguely *familiar*.

"Did you drop it again?" asked Declan when she didn't rise.

"I did, but—"

She reached back under the seat, her fingers just brushing the edge of the white object she'd spotted. It was a piece of metal, flat, with rounded edges, wedged against the side of the seat.

"There's something else stuck in here."

"More jewelry?"

"No, it's metal, but..."

After pushing and tugging the object in several different directions, the thin metal plate gave way, and Charlotte slid it out to shine her flashlight on the face of it.

Her jaw fell slack.

"What is it?"

She looked up at him. "It's...*mine*."

Declan craned his neck, trying to catch a glimpse of what she held in her hand. "What do you mean?"

Charlotte stared at the small aluminum rectangle. The shape and design of it mimicked a Florida license plate, but instead of random letters and numbers, the name *Charlotte* had been pressed into it and painted black.

She turned the thin sheet of pressed metal around so Declan could see it.

"It's my license plate. I used to have it on the back of my tricycle."

Declan took it from her, scowling.

"I don't understand. How did it get here?"

Charlotte stood and slid back in the driver's seat, goosebumps rising on her arm. "Bob said my mother used to have a car like this. He said my grandmother sold it after she died."

Declan handed her back the toy license plate. "You're saying this is your mother's car?"

Charlotte felt her cheeks flush. Her eyes began to tear, and she wiped at them, looking away. "I'm sorry. I don't know why I'm making a big deal about this."

"Are you kidding?" Declan leaned over and pulled her toward him. "Don't be embarrassed. This is incredible. What were the chances that you'd happen to buy back your mother's car?"

"I was so young when she died. I barely remember her. I didn't even remember this car. Frank had to remind me."

"You must have remembered it subconsciously, maybe?"

"Maybe. I *was* drawn to it."

He kissed her on the top of her head and hugged her close to him. "My gift seems pretty silly now."

She leaned back to peer into his eyes. "What? No, I *love* the earrings."

"Sure, they're cute, but your car just gave you a gift that made you burst into tears."

She laughed, sniffing and feeling a little silly with emotion. "But you were here for me to share this moment. That's the greatest gift at all."

They fell silent for a moment before Declan laughed, and she joined him, hooting.

"You are so cheesy," he said.

She nodded, still laughing. "That was *super* cheesy."

"I can smell cheddar."

"Car smells like a fondue party." Charlotte handed him the plate. "Put this in my glove compartment. It'll be my good luck charm."

He slipped the little license plate into the Volvo's glove compartment and closed it before resting his hand on her leg. "Ready?"

She nodded, checking her makeup in the rearview mirror and wiping away any remnants of tears. She still had a yellowing bruise on her eye from her tussle with Stephanie. All she needed now were red puffy lids and smeared mascara, and she'd be a proper trainwreck.

"Just a sec."

She finished removing her other earrings and replaced them with the pineapples.

"What do you think?" she asked, turning her head from side to side to show them off.

"They look great. But how could they not look amazing on you?"

She squinted at him. "Are you trying to out-cheese me?"

He shook his head. "Never."

She leaned forward to kiss him.

"Ready?" she asked, giving him an extra peck on the tip of his nose.

He eyeballed the bar and took a deep breath. "As I'll ever be."

They hopped out of the car and headed into The Anne Bonny.

Seamus spotted Charlotte just as Declan left her to find them something to drink. Declan's uncle strode across the bar, his arms outstretched.

"Hello, my love! Welcome to The Anne Bonny," he said, thrusting a small copper mug into her hand.

"What's this?" she asked, taking it.

"It's a special grog I made for the party. You'll love it."

"I love what you've done with the place." Charlotte's gaze swept across the dimly lit bar. Pirate paraphernalia hung from every wall and much of the ceiling, but every seat had been claimed by a local eager to experience the new watering hole. It seemed The Anne Bonny would be a hit. Party lights lined the walls and hung from the beams spanning the ceiling.

Seamus looked around the room, grinning. "I think she came together nicely."

"What made you call it The Anne Bonny?"

"The idea came to me in a dream. She's the most famous Irish pirate, you know."

"I did *not* know that." Charlotte took a sip of the grog and winced, her lips puckering. The concoction tasted like it had been mixed in a pirate's sweaty boot.

"What's in this?" she asked, doing her best not to cough. "It can't be legal."

"Can you keep a secret?"

"I'll probably be dead in a second, so sure."

Seamus leaned in. "It's all the old booze the previous owners left behind and some juice they had on sale at Publix."

Charlotte grimaced and put her mug on the bar. "It's worse than being keelhauled."

Seamus shrugged. "Better than throwing all that booze out. That would be *wasteful*."

"I think you've confused *wasteful* with the *right thing to do*."

Seamus took a sip of his own drink, which Charlotte noted was *not* grog.

"So I hear you caught Stephanie up to her neck in it," he said.

Charlotte nodded.

"Rumor is you saw her kill a man."

She sighed. "No. I didn't, *actually*. He was dead when I got there, I think. She says she didn't do it."

"But she shot at you, too."

Charlotte's gaze shot to Seamus. "Where did you hear that?"

Seamus smiled. "I have my sources. Are you pressing charges?"

Charlotte opened her mouth, but no words came forth. She honestly didn't know. The whole event had been so surreal. Now she wondered if she really had heard the clicks of Stephanie's gun.

I did, didn't I?

But to pile on when she was already up for murder...

Why do I feel bad for her? The woman is a nightmare...

Declan appeared behind his uncle with two mugs of punch in his hands, saving the day and leaving her beholden to answer.

"The slug they pulled out of Jason Walsh came from Stephanie's gun," he said, handing Charlotte one of the drinks.

She took the mug and put it directly on the bar beside her other one. "Where did you hear that?"

"Frank just told me. Darla said he's on his fourth glass of punch, and he's chattier than I've ever seen him. He said almost *four* full sentences to me."

Seamus winked at Charlotte. "Fourth glass. See? People love the grog."

Declan glanced at Charlotte's mugs. "I saw you were empty-handed. You didn't want any?" He took a sip of his own mug as he finished his sentence. His expression twisted as if he'd sipped battery acid. Which, Charlotte guessed, he *had* from the taste of it.

"Holy—"

"There's nothing holy about it," said Charlotte, laughing.

"Why didn't you warn me?"

"It wouldn't have been half as much fun."

Charlotte felt her phone vibrate in her pocket and fished it out to check the screen. She didn't recognize the number. She excused herself and stepped outside to escape the Irish music long enough to take the call.

"Hello?"

The voice on the other end of the line was female, but Charlotte couldn't place it.

"Tell them you know she didn't do it."

"What? Who is this?"

"Stephanie's innocent. Tell them."

Charlotte's jaw creaked open, her own voice stolen. A chill ran down her spine.

She recognized the speaker now.

Stephanie's mother, Jamie Moriarty. A voice Charlotte had hoped to never hear again.

That's why I feel bad for her.

The reason Charlotte felt so much misplaced compassion for Stephanie became clear as polished glass.

Stephanie's mother is the notorious Puzzle Killer, possibly the most prolific serial killer of all time.

What chance did Stephanie have? Who was there to teach her love? Charlotte still felt scarred from the *short* time she'd spent hunting—and losing—Jamie Moriarty.

Imagine if she were my mother.

She'd been lucky to escape with her life during Jamie's last visit to Pineapple Port.

"I don't know your daughter's innocent," said Charlotte, embarrassed to hear her voice stick in her suddenly dry throat.

"But you'll find a way to prove it."

"You want *me* to prove Stephanie's innocent?"

"I do."

"Why me?"

Jamie paused. "Why not you? Don't let me down. The consequences would be...*unfortunate.*"

The phone went dead.

Charlotte lowered herself to the step of The Anne Bonny, staring at her phone.

She'd just been threatened by the most notorious serial killer of all time.

That can't be good.

~~ THE END ~~

WANT MORE? FREE PREVIEW!

If you liked this book, read on for a preview of the next Pineapple Port Mystery AND the Shee McQueen Mystery-Thriller Series (which shares characters with the Pineapple Port world!).

THANK YOU!

Thank you for reading! If you enjoyed this book, please swing back to Amazon and leave me a review — even short reviews help authors like me find new fans!

ABOUT THE AUTHOR

USA Today and *Wall Street Journal* bestselling author Amy Vansant has written over 30 books, including the fun, thrilling Shee McQueen series, the rollicking, twisty Pineapple Port Mysteries, and the action-packed Kilty urban fantasies. She's also the founder of AuthorsXP.com – a site for authors (marketing help) and readers (free and deal books!).

Amy lives in Jupiter, Florida, with her muse/husband and a goony Bordoodle named Archer.

http://www.AmyVansant.com

FOLLOW AMY on AMAZON or BOOKBUB

BOOKS BY AMY VANSANT

Pineapple Port Mysteries
Funny, clean & full of unforgettable characters
Shee McQueen Mystery-Thrillers
Action-packed, fun romantic mystery-thrillers
Kilty Urban Fantasy/Romantic Suspense
Action-packed romantic suspense/urban fantasy
Slightly Romantic Comedies
Classic romantic romps
The Magicatory
Middle-grade fantasy

FREE PREVIEW

PINEAPPLE

JAILBIRD

A Pineapple Port Mystery: Book Eight – By
Amy Vansant

Chapter One

Christmas lights blinked on almost every lamppost of Charlotte's street, their cheery twinkling curving into the distance like an airport runway constructed by someone deep into the spiked eggnog. Yawning and stretching for the stars, Charlotte strolled to the base of her driveway to grab the morning paper. Her movement triggered a neighbor's motion-activated Santa into a series of muffled ho-ho-hos. Santa's voice had been failing him as the season waned.

Christmas had been over for a week, but people loved the holidays in Pineapple Port, the fifty-five-plus neighborhood where Charlotte had grown up. The residents dragged out the season until every plastic reindeer on every roof *begged* to be stuffed back into the garage. Many of the locals still had family visiting—sons and daughters and grandkids who didn't want to go back to the freezing Northeast. Or freezing Midwest. Or, heaven forbid, *Canada.*

It made Charlotte shiver just thinking about those places. She had Florida blood. A temperature dip into the fifties was enough to send her scurrying for a snowsuit and gloves. She was a newly minted, fully licensed private investigator, but how people survived winter north of Florida was a mystery she didn't think she'd ever solve.

Luckily, the thermometers hovered at sixty-seven this December morning—

Charlotte cocked her head.

Hold on. That's not right.

As her fingers grazed the top of her bagged newspaper, the

house across the street caught her attention. Mariska lived there with her husband, Bob. Mariska had raised Charlotte after her grandmother died, leaving Charlotte the only permanent resident of Pineapple Port under the age of fifty-five. She'd already been orphaned before moving in with her grandmother, and if Mariska and the other residents hadn't worked the system for her, she would have been thrown into the custody of the state.

Thanks to Mariska, instead of being shuffled from one foster home to another, Charlotte had spent her days wheeling around the neighborhood in a golf cart and shuffling through water aerobics until her fingertips puckered.

Charlotte knew all Mariska's tics and habits and this morning, something wasn't *right*. She knew what the house across the street was supposed to look like at five a.m. because her dog, Abby, who *used* to fetch the paper, had developed the playful habit of tearing the news to shreds before dragging the remnants back to the door, newspaper streaming behind her like she was a furry parade float.

Charlotte didn't want to fire Abby from her only job, but piecing the paper together so she could read it wasn't easy before her coffee.

The new morning ritual involved Charlotte tootling down the driveway to grab her paper while Abby wandered off to do her business. During this time, Mariska's lights were always on.

Today, Mariska's lights were *off*.

Mariska and Bob took turns waking up too early—he had to go to the bathroom, her legs ached—there was always something.

But the lights weren't on today.

This morning, Mariska didn't wave at her through the window, holding up her dog, Izzy, and working the mutt's paw so it looked as if the pointy-eared shedding machine was waving as well. That wasn't *too* strange—Mariska hadn't held up Miss Izzy in a while. The dog had grown into a sturdy *brick* of hair and weighed about as much as a small pickup truck thanks to Mariska's inability to stop treating her.

But it wasn't just the lack of lights and waving dog paws bothering Charlotte.

She took a step to the left, still peering at Mariska's door.

There it is.

Mariska's door was *ajar.* She hadn't registered the shadow at first but now she could see the front door of Mariska's double-wide pre-fab home appeared to be hanging at an angle. A trick of the light. The door was simply open.

Charlotte straightened, paper hanging in her hand, until Abby flew by, snatching it from her grasp. The Soft-coated Wheaten gave her prize a good shaking and tore at the plastic sleeve until the paper unfurled like a flag across the driveway. Abby immediately lost interest, spat out the plastic, and returned to sniffing around the yard.

Charlotte sighed and stared at Mariska's daily news, still lying at the end of her driveway. If she or Bob had come outside to fetch it, and left the door open, they hadn't finished the job.

Izzy didn't fetch papers. Mariska's dog preferred to stay inside and protect the family from animals on the television set, barking and rushing to slam her nose into the screen whenever a critter appeared in a commercial. She particularly hated a cartoon eagle that mocked her from the screen as she yapped and tried to circle behind the television to find it.

Charlotte took another step toward Mariska's home.

Maybe they went around the back...

She wandered a few feet down the street to peer around the side of Mariska's house.

Nothing. But wait—

Mariska's golf cart wasn't in her driveway.

Charlotte sighed.

Well, there it is.

At least one of them went somewhere on the golf cart. Mystery solved.

Charlotte looked at her watch as she turned back toward her house, only to make a full three-sixty and head straight for Mariska's, her pace quickening.

It was five o'clock in the morning.

Why would they go somewhere on the golf cart at this hour? Was something wrong?

She whistled for the Wheaton to follow and Abby appeared at her heels, excited to break morning tradition and head to Mariska's house early.

Abby *loved* that woman and her treats.

Charlotte grabbed Mariska's paper on her way past, partially to be helpful, but mostly to keep Abby from temptation. She peered through Mariska's glass storm door, but couldn't see much. The entranceway opened into a narrow hall. Everything inside sat still and dark.

She opened the storm door and called inside past the open internal door, her voice low and whispery.

"Mariska?"

Izzy barreled around the corner, slipping on the linoleum floor, landing on her hip and springing back up to continue her approach. She whined, knocking the door open wider as she pressed her nose through, whip-like tail wagging.

Charlotte opened the storm door far enough for Abby to charge into the house, her broad chest bouncing off Izzy's head. Izzy pirouetted and trotted after the Wheaton as the two of them scrambled room-to-room—Abby investigating and Izzy following to make sure her nosy neighbor didn't touch her stuff.

Charlotte entered and peeked into the open-plan kitchen and living room. Bob wasn't sitting in his worn La-Z-Boy chair. She walked through to check the lanai and found the sliding door leading to it closed and locked. Mariska opened the sliding door every morning because Izzy's water bowl was kept in the lanai, an arrangement made necessary by Izzy's inability to drink without throwing water around the room like a sprinkler.

If the door isn't open, Mariska isn't up.

Staring down the hallway that led to the bedrooms, Charlotte weighed the pros and cons of creeping back there. Her presence already felt like an invasion of privacy. Entering Mariska's bedroom would be even worse, but something didn't feel right and she couldn't leave until she knew everything was okay.

Entering unnaturally still houses in a fifty-five-plus community didn't always end well, but there was no way Mariska *and* Bob both had heart attacks overnight. Charlotte pushed the morbid thought out of her head.

Let's get this over with so I can get back to my coffee.

Charlotte tiptoed down the hall as the dogs barreled from the spare room and headed back toward the kitchen, nearly taking out her kneecaps in the process.

"Mariska?"

The bedroom door was ajar. The room behind it was darker than the hallway, which bathed in ambient light from the nightlight plugged into the guest bathroom wall.

"Bob?"

Charlotte poked her head into the room and tried to focus on the bed. It looked as if someone was in there.

Good. They're still sleeping.

Maybe they accidentally left the door open last night after walking Izzy.

Huffing a sigh, Charlotte was about to turn and leave when a tickle scurried across the nape of her neck.

Something about the lumps in the bed.

They weren't *lumpy* enough.

Charlotte poked her head back into the bedroom. She couldn't hear anyone snoring. Her eyes adjusted to the darkness until she could see something in the air above the sleeping bodies.

A hand?

One of the sleepers had their hand in the air, thrust up like a redwood tree, as if a teacher asked a question and they had the answer.

How can someone sleep with their hand in the air?

"Mariska?"

The arm was skinny.

Very skinny.

That shape of arm didn't belong to Mariska or Bob. But now her eyes were adjusting to the dark and she could see the fingers at the end of the arm clear as day.

It was definitely a hand.

The time had come to abandon polite caution. Charlotte slapped at the switch on the wall and the room flooded with light.

She gasped.

Eyes stared back at her.

Unblinking.

The four eyes were *painted* on the faces of the two mannequins occupying Mariska and Bob's bed. Both wore wigs vaguely resembling Bob and Mariska's hair, but nothing else about them rang true. One of them had a permanently straight arm thrust into the air. Something hung looped around that mannequin's frozen thumb, a red ribbon holding an envelope aloft where it dangled against its wrist.

Charlotte moved to the envelope and lifted the ribbon.

Fingerprints.

Sheriff Frank would kill her if she messed up the evidence.

Charlotte ran to the en-suite bathroom and searched under the sink through piles of decorative soaps and cleaning products until she found cleaning gloves. She slipped them on and returned to the bedroom to pull the envelope from the mannequin's grasp.

The envelope proved un-licked, its flap tucked neatly into itself. She slipped it open with her clumsy rubber-sheathed thumb and retrieved a small note from inside.

The white slip of paper held a single sentence scrawled across it.

This is what it feels like to lose someone.

—Jamie

Chapter Two

"My name is Solomon Black. I've been retained to represent you, Ms. Moriarty."

Stephanie scowled at the man across the table from her. She'd been called from her prison cell to meet with her lawyer.

Thing was, she didn't have a lawyer.

The man claiming to be her lawyer looked wealthy and well-put-together in his expensive bespoke suit and gold cufflinks, but the pallor of his face looked as if he'd been throwing up all morning. He appeared wealthy—a fancy lawyer—but not one feeling particularly strong.

She tucked a straggly blonde strand behind her ear. The hard water in the prison showers was *murdering* her hair.

"You don't look so good," she said.

Solomon reached into his pocket and thrust a phone toward her. "I have a phone call for you."

The thin sheen of sweat on his brow glistened under the meeting room's harsh lighting.

Hm.

The expensive suit, the fear on his face, the sweat...the math of Solomon Black's appearance was beginning to add up.

Stephanie looked at the phone.

I know who that is.

She took the phone and placed it against her ear.

"Hello, Mother."

"Did you do it?" said a voice on the other side of the line.

"No. I didn't."

Her mother, Jamie, grunted.

"You sound like you don't believe me."

"I've kept tabs on you. I know you *could* have done it."

"Yes, I *could* have, but I didn't. First of all, it was sloppy. Four people showed up in that warehouse after the shooting. I don't usually kill someone and then sell tickets."

Solomon rolled his eyes and looked away. Stephanie held her hand over the phone and whispered to him.

"Hypothetically speaking."

He nodded. "Of course."

Jamie chuckled. "Tickets. I never thought of that. I could have made a fortune."

Stephanie sniffed. "Anyway, I don't do that sort of thing anymore," she mumbled.

"Since when?"

"Since about two weeks ago, if you must know."

"Oh yes? What happened two weeks ago?"

Stephanie sighed. "I was *inspired*."

"Inspired by whom?"

"I'd rather not say."

"Tell me."

"Declan."

"Declan? The local boy? Since when does he inspire you?"

"Since now. In a way, his new girlfriend did too."

Jamie laughed. "His new girlfriend? That relationship will last about ten minutes after you get out of jail. You two are like peas in a pod."

"No, that's just it, Mom. We're not. You might think you keep tabs on me but you don't know me and you don't know Declan. He's...he's not like *us*."

"I know, but he's like a puppy following you around."

"No, he's not. He never was."

"He went to South America with you and your little death squad."

"And he left as soon as things went south. He tried to get me to leave with him. He wasn't following me. He was trying to save me from myself."

Jamie grunted. "How noble. And this new girlfriend. Why her?"

"Why is he dating her?"

"No, why did *she* inspire you?"

"I don't know. She's a drip."

"Sounds inspiring."

"No..." Stephanie paused to think for a moment. "I suppose in some ways, she reminds me of me, only *good*."

"What do you mean *good*?"

"She's *good*. It's like she's Superman and I'm...who's the bad superman?"

"Clark Kent?"

"No, Clark Kent is his mild-mannered persona. I feel like there was a *bad* Superman. Wasn't there?"

"I really couldn't tell you."

Stephanie held the phone down and addressed Solomon.

"Who's the bad Superman?"

Solomon paled another shade. "I don't know. Do I have to know? I could make a call—"

Stephanie shook her head and waved him away. "Nevermind." She raised the phone back to her ear. "You get the idea."

"Yes. *Bad Superman* is pretty self-explanatory. You're saying she's the super hero and you're the super villain."

"I guess."

Stephanie shifted in the uncomfortable metal chair. Talking to her mother was always humiliating. She couldn't understand why she didn't cut the woman out of her life completely, the way Jamie had cut her out of *her* life shortly after birth. She guessed it was a little too late to hand her mother over to some Florida trailer trash.

Or maybe too *early*.

Her mother would have to get old someday. Maybe she could put her in a home with *really* low standards...

"Are you there?"

Stephanie snapped from her daydreaming. "Huh? Yes. I'm here. What do you want, anyway? And who's this guy?" Her attention settled on the lawyer and he seemed to melt beneath her gaze.

Solomon cleared his throat. "I told you, my name is Solomon Black and I've been retained—"

Stephanie glared at the man and he shut his mouth.

"He's your lawyer. He's the best. He's from New York."

"You bought me a lawyer?"

"Bought? In a manner of speaking. Let's just say things won't work out well for *him* if he doesn't get you off."

Ah. That explains why he looks like he's about to hurl on me.

"But you didn't even know I was innocent."

Jamie scoffed. "Like *that* matters. I'm a little disappointed you're not, to be honest."

"Does this mean you care about me?"

Jamie's playful tone dissipated. "You know who I am and you have my DNA. I can't have you in the prison system with nothing to do but think of ways to bargain your way to freedom."

Stephanie frowned. "Stop. You're gushing. It's embarrassing."

"Just tell Solomon everything you can think of to help him find you a way out."

"Well, I didn't kill Jason, so this should be his easiest case ever."

"You *said* you shot at him."

"In self-defense."

"Even so, Steph, it's not looking good. It isn't a coincidence you ended up in that warehouse. Someone set you up."

"But I didn't kill him. He was already in that chair, dead—"

"Tell Solomon everything. And when he gets you out from under these charges, you and I will have a talk about your new life plan. That is, if Declan's okay with that."

Jamie spat the word Declan as if it tasted bad in her mouth.

"New life plan? What—"

The air on the other side of the line stopped its subtle hissing and Stephanie knew the connection had been severed. She handed the phone back to Solomon.

"Your mother wants you to tell me—"

Stephanie held up her palm. "I know."

She wanted to ask her fancy new lawyer what her mother had threatened to do to him if he didn't win her case, but decided it didn't matter. Her psychopath mother would do anything to get what she wanted and this time, what she wanted was to know her daughter wouldn't help the authorities find her.

A chill ran down Stephanie's spine.

She thinks I'm a liability.

It was never a good idea to be a liability in Jamie's world.

It could be prison was the only thing keeping her alive. But trapped here, there was little she could do to hide. Who knew how far her mother's influence reached?

I'll need to stay on my toes.

Jamie's regrets didn't tend to live very long.

Get *Pineapple Jailbird* on Amazon!

ANOTHER FREE PREVIEW!

THE GIRL WHO WANTS

A Shee McQueen Mystery-Thriller by Amy Vansant

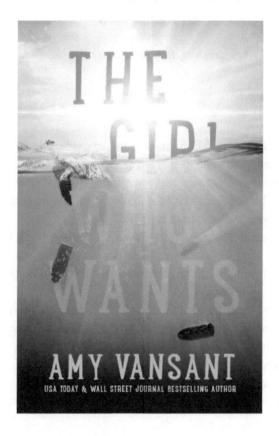

CHAPTER ONE

Three Weeks Ago, Nashua, New Hampshire.

Shee realized her mistake the moment her feet left the grass.

He's enormous.

She'd watched him drop from the side window of the house. He landed four feet from where she stood, and still her brain refused to register the warning signs. The nose, big and lumpy as breadfruit, the forehead some beach town could use as a jetty if they buried him to his neck...

His knees bent to absorb his weight, and *her* brain thought, *got you.*

Her brain couldn't be bothered with simple math: *Giant, plus Shee, equals Pain.*

Instead, she jumped to tackle him, dangling airborne as his knees straightened and the *pet the rabbit* bastard stood to his full height.

Crap.

The math added up pretty quickly after that.

Hovering like Superman mid-flight, there wasn't much she

could do to change her disastrous trajectory. She'd *felt* like a superhero when she left the ground. Now, she felt more like a Canada goose staring into the propellers of Captain Sully's Airbus A320.

She might take down the plane, but it was going to *hurt*.

Frankenjerk turned toward her at the same moment she plowed into him. She clamped her arms around his waist like a little girl hugging a redwood. Lurch returned the embrace, twisting her to the ground. Her back hit the dirt, and air burst from her lungs like a double shotgun blast.

Ow.

Wheezing, she punched upward, striking Beardless Hagrid in the throat.

That didn't go over well.

Grabbing her shoulder with one hand, Dickasaurus flipped her on her stomach like a sausage link, slipped his hand under her chin, and pressed his forearm against her windpipe.

The only air she'd gulped before he cut her supply stank of damp armpit. He'd tucked her cranium in his arm crotch, much like the famous noggin-less horseman once held his severed head. Fireworks exploded in the dark behind her eyes.

That's when a thought occurred to her.

I haven't been home in fifteen years.

What if she died in Gigantor's armpit? Would her father even know?

Has it really been that long?

Flopping like a landed fish, she forced her assailant to adjust his hold and sucked a breath as she flipped on her back. Spittle glistened on his lips, his brow furrowed as if she'd asked him to read a paragraph of big-boy words.

His nostrils flared like the Holland Tunnel.

There's an idea.

Making a V with her fingers, Shee thrust upward, stabbing into his nose, straining to reach his tiny brain.

Goliath roared. Jerking back, he grabbed her arm to unplug her fingers from his nose socket. She whipped away her limb before he had a good grip, fearing he'd snap her bones with his

Godzilla paws.

Kneeling before her, he clamped both hands over his face, cursing as blood seeped from behind his fingers.

Shee's gaze didn't linger on that mess. Her focus fell to his crotch, hovering a foot above her feet, protected by nothing but a thin pair of oversized sweatpants.

Scrambled eggs, sir?

She kicked.

He howled.

Shee scuttled back like a crab, found her feet, and snatched her gun from her side. The gun she should have pulled *before* trying to tackle the Empire State Building.

"Move a muscle, and I'll aerate you," she said. She always liked that line.

The golem growled but remained on the ground like a good dog, cradling his family jewels.

Shee's partner in this manhunt, a local cop easier on the eyes than he was useful, rounded the corner and drew his own weapon.

She smiled and holstered the gun he'd lent her. Unknowingly.

"Glad you could make it."

Her portion of the operation accomplished, she headed toward the car as more officers swarmed the scene.

"Shee, where are you going?" called the cop.

She stopped and turned.

"Home, I think."

His gaze dropped to her hip.

"Is that my gun?"

Get *The Girl Who Wants* on Amazon!

Made in United States
Troutdale, OR
12/02/2023